Reading *Wine*

And other Short Stories and Poems

The Winners Anthology

For the

2011 Christian Writing Contest

Hosted by

Athanatos Christian Ministries

I0685787

ATHANATOS
PUBLISHING GROUP

Reading Wine And Other Stories and Poems: The Winners Anthology for the 2011 Athanatos Christian Ministries Christian Writing Contest.

2011 Christian Writing Contest
www.christianwritingcontest.com

Copyright 2011, by Athanatos Christian Ministries
www.athanatosministries.org

Published by the Athanatos Publishing Company
www.athanatosministries.org/group

Cover by Julius Broqueza

1st Edition, Paperback.

ISBN-13: 978-0-9822776-8-3

Printed in the United States of America.

Table of Contents

Honorable Mentions
(not included in the anthology)

Poetry Category

The Francis Thompson Award:
Lynn Brookside -*When Clouds Were Carousels*
The George Herbert Award:
Chris Dickinson – *Scripture Sonnets(5)*

19 and Up Category

Leo Tolstoy Award:
Erika Castiglione – ***Hope Rising***
The William Shakespeare Award:
Richard Denhard –***Childish Ways***

High School Category

The Graham Greene Award:
Cody Milner-*Claudius Marcus Lysias*
The Charles Williams Award:
Nathaniel Rebiger- *The Gift*

ATHANATOS
CHRISTIAN MINISTRIES

Athanatos Christian Ministries is proud to release this anthology containing the winners' entries of its third annual Christian writing contest. As an apologetics organization, ACM designed the contest with the desire to raise up Christian authors who could reflect the Christian worldview through written narrative. With so many voices influencing opinions, hearts, and attitudes, and the stakes as high as they are, ACM believes that it is more important than ever to have Christians involved in the conversation.

This doesn't always mean hitting people over the head with the Bible or 'God Talk.' Sometimes, it just means giving people a new perspective. Sometimes, it just means showing Christians can laugh. This anthology provides examples of several approaches and ACM is proud to put them all on display.

ACM would like to thank all of the judges and sponsors for their help in making this contest possible, and of course Jesus Christ, the Word.

To read the 2011 winning entries online and learn more about future contests, please visit:
www.christianwritingcontest.com

In Christ,

Anthony Horvath
Executive Director
Athanatos Christian Ministries, Inc.

2011 Contest Sponsors:

www.christianwritingcontest.com

Athanatos Christian Ministries

www.athanatosministries.org

Confident Christianity

www.confidentchristianity.com

Hieropraxis

www.hieropraxis.com

Christian Manuscript Submission.com

www.christianmanuscriptsubmissions.com

Author Joseph Keysor
Hitler, the Holocaust, and the Bible

www.hitlerandchristianity.com

Wisdom's Gate

www.wisdomsgate.com

Sojourner Leatherwork

Hieropraxis

is proud to present the 2011

Gerard Manley Hopkins Award

1st Place

and the

T.S. Eliot Award

2nd Place

To Donna Frisinger for

Permanent Houseguest* and *Bullets for a Hometown Hero

(Category: Poetry)

Bio:

Like her childhood hero, Peter Pan, who never wanted to grow up, **Donna Austgen-Frisinger** has determined to carry a little fairy dust with her at all times as a constant reminder to view life through a child's eyes. Today, as a mid-career freelancer who still believes she can fly (via her retro-look Schwinn bicycle, *complete* with handlebar streamers and ringing bell), her life experiences — as a band director's wife of forty years, school teacher, performing arts director, dance team coach, Christian bookstore clerk, music minister/evangelist with the International Church of the Foursquare Gospel, and mentor to thousands of kids — all serve her well in her writing career, as she uses her God-given talents to script fresh tales of His Kingdom through creative prose and poetry for both children and adults.

www.donnafrisinger.com

I fled Him down the nights and down the days;
I fled Him, down the arches of the years;
I fled Him, down the labyrinthine ways
Of my own mind; and in the midst of tears.

"The Hound of Heaven"
Francis Thompson, 1859-1907)

PERMANENT HOUSEGUEST

Donna Frisinger

Hound of Heaven, pursue my friend; lavishly lick her face.
Please make her giggle, restore her soul, and nuzzle her with grace
To cover wounds in blameless-bliss, beguiling puppy whines,
As balm to heal the ravages defined by Hell's designs

To cripple and ensnare her in deceptions of the past,
The lies of devils -- meant to keep her prisoner and outcast,
When all she yearns for is to feel the warmth of your sweet breath;
Track down my friend, with panting thirst, who's hitchhiking with death.

Keep scampering, yelping, yipping and just nipping at her heels,
To trip her up and knock her down, until she finally kneels,
Reminding her she's royalty -- this princess in disguise --
Who wrestles with the Hound of Love through tears of blinded eyes,

Enticing her to hug you close, embrace your racing heart,
Forgetting and forgiving all that's tearing her apart,
Adoring, as a newborn babe, held captive by your rest,
To snuggle and invite you stay as permanent houseguest.

BULLETS FOR A HOMETOWN HERO

Donna Frisinger

War and its horrors
are nothing more than a
blip on the nightly news. Another
R-Rated movie on the silver screen, *until*
personal loss translates its reality into your
own living room. The fictitious security of buttered
popcorn, diet coke, and the TV remote suddenly crashes
to the floor when that detached picture show is
interrupted by the doorbell: "I'm sorry to
inform you that your husband, daddy,
lover, best friend has been killed
in the line of duty.

That's it. Gone are
cuddles, kisses, shared
jokes, quirky idiosyncrasies, hand
squeezes ... No more "I'm sorry. See
ya later! What time will you be home? Be
careful! Have you seen my keys? Let the dog out.
Where's the checkbook? Remember the ballgame,
recital, play practice ... Don't forget the trash.
Her diaper needs changed. Daddy's home!
How was your day? I need a hug.
Love you; right back at ya.
Do you have to go?"

A parade of strangers,
well-meaning friends, converge
at my front door to plan a good-bye
that doesn't even seem real. What is the
protocol? Who should be called? Included?
This is bigger than my numb and empty arms. But
he is a hometown hero, after-all, and they want to do
it right. Top-notch. Center-stage. Befitting this
man who shared my deepest secrets, my
bed, my heartaches, my uncertainties,
imagined (and very real) fears.
My fondest memories.

3

No time for questions:
"How? When? Where? Why
him?" *But, he was coming home!* What
will I do without him? How do I take another
step forward? My legs are wooden. Keep breathing,
moving, watching, waiting, yearning, praying, hoping ,
expecting. *Maybe they made a mistake!* It's been known
to happen. What about the kids? They need their
father. I need my soul-mate. And the tears
come again, just when I thought the
well had been spent. How
can I possibly go on?

A whispering
in my soul, a gentle nudge:
"I Am with you always, even to
the end of time. I will not leave you or
forsake you. I Am a husband to the widow; your
strength, shelter, ever-present help in time of trouble.
I Am your all-in-all. *Nothing* can separate you from
my love. I give my angels charge over you to
guard you in all your ways. I Am the
Resurrection and the Life. He who
lives and believes in Me
Shall *never* die ..."

And so I walk
through this valley with
hope in my heart. No mortar barrage,
land mine, bullet, car bomb, or sniper can
rob me of the deep assurance flooding my heart
in this quiet hour. There *is* peace, victory -- even in the
midst of my greatest sorrow, because of an empty tomb
vacated by Heaven's own Home-Town-Hero. "He is
risen!" the angel said. "He is not here." And
because He lives, my beloved lives,
waiting for me on the other side
of this ticking clock.

Athanatos Christian Ministries

is proud to present the 2011

John Donne Award

3rd Place

To

Sharlyn Guthrie for *Creation's Song*

(Category: Poetry)

Bio:

I enjoy writing poetry, devotionals, and short stories, especially those that honor my Lord and Savior. I am a preschool teacher in Iowa, as well as the director of education and music for a U.S. based ministry to Uganda. Music, biking, and gardening are some of my pastimes when I am not traveling or spending time with my family. My husband, John, and I have three married sons and six beautiful grandchildren. http://dancinonrainbows.blogspot.com/

Creation's Song

Sharlyn Guthrie
All Rights Reserved

Oh mystical, musical Presence
without beginning or end,
voice of three, yet One in its essence:
a lilting tenor of wind
over bass booming thunderous and wild
by pure tones of the Word reconciled.

Oh Voice shaking all the foundations
of what was yet to be made
in harmonious, pure undulations
as base and ballast were laid.
Great I AM moves with tremulous sweep
chanting, "Let there be…" into the deep.

Holy, Holy, Holy is the Lord God, Almighty,
Who was and Who is and Who is to come!

Oh Composer of body and spirit
forged in the image of God,
so to honor God's Word and to fear it
while ruling the beasts and sod,
orchestrating their care and provision
in sync with the Master Musician.

Oh Creator of holy acclaim
Who over creation stood,
poised to view Your work and proclaim,
"Behold, it is very good!"
then led morning stars in their singing
with shouts of glad angel choirs ringing.

Holy, Holy, Holy is the Lord God, Almighty,
Who was and Who is and Who is to come!

Oh high, humorous Virtuoso,
maker of rhythm and rhyme,
Who transcribes creature noises in scherzo,
varied in tempo and time;
then in cycles of life stays their course
by intrinsic, intuitive force.

Oh immanent, sovereign Conductor,
arranger of varied parts,
blending anthems and hymns in nature
to the trill of lovers' hearts.
Trees clap softly to meadowlark's song
as a cadence of crickets plays on.

Holy, Holy, Holy is the Lord God, Almighty,
Who was and Who is and Who is to come!

Oh Maestro of mercy and justice,
the sweetest duet by far,
born of flesh, yet holy and blameless,
now branded with Satan's scar.
Yet the dirge became jubilation;
You rose, and proclaimed vindication.

Oh infinite, timeless Transposer
tuning each age to Your grace,
preparing to slay the imposer
and then to reveal Your face,
when our crowns at Your feet have been laid
and the great final movement is played.

Holy, Holy, Holy is the Lord God, Almighty,
Who was and Who is and Who is to come!

*Refrain is borrowed from Revelation 4:8 (NASV)

Athanatos Christian Ministries

is proud to present the 2011

C.S. Lewis Award

To

Robert Cely

West Columbia, S. Carolina

1st Place

(Category: 19 and up)

Bio:

Robert is a thirty-six year old native of Columbia, South Carolina, where he currently resides with his four children and his one wife, the radiant Elizabeth Cely. He has the immense privilege of being employed as a Chaplain for Amedisys Hospice, where he has served the spiritual needs of dying patients for the last three years. Robert fell in love with writing at a young age and has remained entranced by the power of a good story ever since. He loves to refer to himself in the third person

Reading Wine

Robert Cely

Most people believe I am magic. That's what it looks like to them at least. But to me it comes as natural as breathing, reading the wine.

I didn't name it reading wine. Other men who saw what I do called it reading wine and the name stuck. I guess that's how things go. I guess that's how people try to grasp what they really don't understand. They slap a label on it as if a name says it all. Never mind that most of our names are useless anyway. That's how they think at least, you name something and you've got it figured out.

Like reading wine.

I just call it tasting. Then again, everyone calls it tasting, and everyone claims to do it. But I found out real early in life that no one can do what I do.

I can assure you that all I do is taste. I can't read wine like I read a newspaper or you are reading these words. I simply let the wine dance across my palate and I can taste every drop of rain, every ray of sunshine, the tilt of the earth, the coolness of the air, even the dirt on the hands that picked the grape. It all jumps out on my tongue in an instant. I promise it's nothing magical. All I do is taste.

By now you've probably figured out who I am, or rather, who I was. Leo the Amazing Wine Reader I was called. Without effort I became the world's most renown food and wine critic.

Yes, I can do it with food too. So of course I became a total food snob as well as popular critic. But it wasn't always for the wrong reasons. With the kind of gift I have you can only eat free range chicken if you eat chicken at all. It is simply impossible to force down even the finest roasted hen when all I can taste is the feces the bird waded through while penned up in the dark its entire six weeks of life. Conventional vegetables are their own trial. All I can taste of them is the powdery and antiseptic flavor of pesticides.

Wine, by far, is the true tasters delight. Most people never experience the true complexity of taste. And to understand wine is to understand what taste truly is.

With practice and training anyone can taste a lot in wine, can discover some of the complexities of the drink. I can taste everything. And I mean everything. With one sip I can tell you not only the type of wine it is, but also the year, the location and every single condition that went into that wine from seed all the way to shipping. I even once tasted a wine that had been heavily jostled or jarred. The amused and incredulous wine merchant scoffed at me until he discovered that the delivery truck had, in fact, been in a wreck, and the bottle I tasted was from one of the few cases that survived intact.

9

I am always on the search for that one, exquisite taste of wine. My whole body anticipates it whenever I open a new bottle and the aroma drifts into me. It is wonder as well as excitement. What is the story of this wine, I ask myself. What are all the subtle parts that went in to making this vintage?

Deep down I am looking for the ultimate wine. I want to savor that draft that holds everything within it, that when I taste it, I will know peace. It may sound strange to hear me say this about wine, but you do not know wine as I do. There is, however, something in your life that is like this, that drives you and has you searching.

Maybe you are a builder who longs to build that perfect house, a lawyer waiting for the case that will define your career, a musician who writes songs until he writes that one that he knows he is truly capable of. Whatever it is that drives you, that has you searching, longing, expecting, it doesn't change the fact that we are all driven to search, we are all driven by thirst.

What I thirst for is a wine that can fulfill the potential of wine. It holds so much in it, but there has never been a wine I have tasted, no matter how full and rich it was, that did not have an emptiness to it. It is hard to explain, but in every wine I can taste something missing, some element, some flavor, and essence that I know should be there though I don't know what it is.

During my first trip to Europe I tasted the legendary 1945 Chateau Mouton-Rothschild. A mentor of mine, an Italian we all called Santi, pulled a bottle from his labyrinthine cellar of old, dusty bottles one night.

"I have been waiting many years for this," Santi told me as we sat on his balcony covered by a Roman night. "But you are the only one who can truly appreciate this. I have never seen a palate such as yours. You were made to taste this wine."

He looked at the bottle longingly, studying its worn label by the moonlight. He was scared to open it. Perhaps the anticipation would eclipse the reality.

"No one can say for sure what makes this wine extraordinary," Santi mused as he carefully poured our glasses. "1945 was a banner year for wine. No one knows why. Maybe you can tell us."

As I drank that first swallow of '45 Rothschild I felt giddy. This was, after all, considered one of the finest ever made. And it certainly was exquisite. I could taste an ideal year of sun and shade, a gentle rain, a goodness in the soil and careful cultivation. But there was something else.

I had tasted it before yet always found it too subtle to identify. It would escape my taste buds just before I could recognize it, slipping away like a phantom from the corner of my eyes.

As I let this legendary wine roll over my tongue the elusive taste screamed out at me, filled the wine, burst from it.

What made the 1945 Mouton-Rothschild so incredible is that it tasted like hope. There was no doubting it. I could taste hope in that wine.

It all makes sense if you think about it. It's what makes wine so incredible. A wine will absorb everything around it. They call it the *terroir*, or lay of the earth. Everything that surrounds a wine gives it a unique taste. Until then I didn't know how much.

In 1945 the land had been liberated from a terrible evil. The Nazis had been pushed back and the people rejoiced. The people were full of hope, and that hope bled into the wine. Even the earth itself was joyful, I could taste it in that wine. There is no doubt that it is the sweet savor of hope that makes 1945 such a wonderful year for wine.

People always ask me if that was the best wine I ever tasted. They are always surprised that it isn't the Mouton-Rothschild, and even more surprised when I tell them what was the best. The best wine I ever tasted was from a little vineyard in Chile, a wine that hardly sold beyond the nearest town. You would have never heard of it.

The wine came from an obscure, family winery. I discovered it while traveling through the Chilean wine country for a wine guide I had been commissioned to write. I saw the little plastic sign pitched on the side of the road and stopped on impulse. The vintner was a stooped old man, his face hidden by wrinkles and his voice hoarse and trembling.

Yet there was a sparkle of joy in him as he showed me his estate. Sometimes he would reach out and lovingly caress the vines we passed by. With impeccable patience he walked me through his cellars and spoke gently in his thick accent about wine.

Finally he let me sample, and it was heaven. At first it only

11

tasted like a simple yet elegant wine. The oak and earth accents were obvious, though not overwhelming. It followed with an exotic taste that sent strange bouquets through my head. And just as these tastes faded, touching my tongue with a musky finish, something incredible happened.

The '45 Rothschild took on the feelings of hope that surrounded it. This wine, this humble Chilean vintage had all that and more. It was more subtle and at the same time more profound and powerful. A warmth suffused through me, like sunshine in the middle of winter. I tasted a depth of the deepest earth, a richness of a thousand flavors, a feeling that swelled up from my heart and into my head.

I tasted love.

From this obscure vineyard I could taste the love that the old man poured into his wine, as if it were made from a part of his very self. I tasted every second of patience, every caress of the grapes, every detail that he employed. But more than that I could taste the pure goodwill for the people for whom he made the wine. He made it for his family and friends, and from that he made love I could taste.

I wept with that first sip. The old vintner smiled as if he knew. And I think he knew what my tears meant. I drank slowly, savoring every blessed drop in my tongue. I felt like I lived his entire life in that glass. When I had finished, I put the glass down and left without a word.

It is rare that I can taste emotion in a wine. On occasion something powerful or primal bursts through. The mouth feel changes such that something delightful or terrible comes through. More often than not it is joy that I taste. I have also detected bitter hints of pride or the sparkle of excitement. When I taste from a new vineyard I can almost always pick up a hint of excitement, as if the vine is full of child-like exuberance. Sometimes I taste sadness or even determination. Only once have I tasted evil. A mere sip and I was nauseous the rest of the night. But the occasions are rare because the emotions must be strong to come out in the wine, even for my taste.

You would think that such an experience would make me

happy; to have a talent such as mine. I imagine some of you are even thinking to yourself how wonderful it would be to have my talent. And yes, it is wonderful. But I am still thirsty. I am always thirsty. There is something missing in the wine that I taste, in all of it, even the ones brimming with emotion. No matter how robust the wine, I can always taste an emptiness. If you still want to insist that I read wine then this emptiness I taste is like finding blank pages in the middle of a book. You see writing before, you see writing after, but something crucial is missing in the middle. I know something is supposed to be there in the wine as surely as if I came across blank pages in the middle of a book. The pages stand for something that should be there, only I don't know what. I only know that I can taste the emptiness.

I could have gone on thirsting forever had it not been for the International Wine Festival in Paris, 2008. There I tasted the most extraordinary, and dare I say, magical, wine that has ever passed over my tongue. For there I finally found the wine that was full.

That night started much like those festivals always did. Here we were, a pack of self-proclaimed elitists, turning our noses up at everything, desperate to find something that no one else likes, eager to trash what most enjoyed, and all the while feeling dizzy with our own sense of superiority and class.

I was their king, and had good reason to be. No one had a palate like mine, and everyone knew it. It filled me with such indescribably smug enjoyment to watch the snobs turn to sycophants when I approached, all of them eager to agree with anything I said about the wine. If any of them had happened to identify a taste before I had tasted that wine then he would absolutely glow with self-delight.

The wines that year were pretty much the same as the previous years. Every year was unique, so there were always different qualities to what I tasted. But the same vineyards showed up year after year. People would try to trick me, and were always disappointed. One man even tried to fool me with some laboratory imitation of La Morachet. I almost gagged on the flavor of plastic and ammonia and sterile solution. His face showed a profound shock at my insight. I knew immediately the swill had been cooked in a lab. The poor scientist didn't know what to make of it. His

13

mind was just too small.

As the event wore on I shooed away the entourage that hounded me. For just a few moments I needed some solitude and fresh air. Outside, the Parisian night smelled of cars and pollution, but if I inhaled through my mouth I could detect the savor of an old world, brim full of human drama.

Coming back into the building I noticed a stall sitting alone in a recess. It was humble and wooden, no banners or decorations or gimmicky giveaways to attract the wayward. It looked like a medieval merchant stall, weathered and full of character. An old man sat there alone, gazing at the crowds that ignored him. He reminded me of my Chilean vintner, the one who put love in his wine, so I sauntered over for sentiment's sake.

"Ah, it's Leo the Amazing Wine Reader," the old man greeted me in a velvety smooth voice that carried undercurrents of sarcasm. "I've been waiting for you."

This was not unusual. Most of the booths at the show eagerly anticipated my appearance. A nod from me was enough to make the Expo a success for any vendor.

"Did you make this?" I asked as the old man poured from a decanter so old the glass had become clouded.

The old man laughed deep with a hint of hidden joy behind it.

"I could never make this," he said. "I am just a salesman."

I wondered at the oddity of one so old still in sales. He didn't have any of the brash charisma a rep usually carried. Quite the contrary, there was an assurance about him as if he could have cared less whether you liked him or his product. But at the same time, his eyes fixed on me as I lifted the glass, and over the rim I could see he was intensely interested in me. He didn't look at me as the other merchants did. They were interested in me because of the way I could hurt or help them. This man stared as if he were interested in me, as if I were deeply valuable to him for a reason I could not fathom.

The old man's eager and care-filled eyes stayed on me as I brought the glass to my lips. His lips parted, mirroring my own motions, anticipating that first taste with me. I smiled at his excitement, such a childish gesture in one so old.

"Drink deeply," he instructed. "Open yourself to it completely."

The wine touched my tongue and at first I thought it was just a bad merlot. I tasted the mild California coast, a cheap grape, overtones of nitrogen fertilizer, migrant worker hands.

I started to remark as such, to wonder aloud why this salesman had come to the Paris Wine Expo to push a ten dollar bottle of grocery store merlot on the world's greatest wine taster, when my palate came alive.

Suddenly, I could taste something older, much older. The Mediterranean sun danced across my taste buds, the salt sea air, an arid but fertile earth. I tasted sawdust from a carpenter's workshop. I tasted miles of endless, burning wilderness. I tasted a storm, a hatred, thousands of sweaty hands pressed close in, putrefaction and then cleanliness, disease and wholeness, crying, pleading, the awe of thousands, the cry of triumph.

Then deeper, a taste soaked deeper into me. I tasted anxiety so acute I felt it myself, a distress I didn't know was humanly possible. The saltiness of sweat and tears filled with cold fear passed through me in a shudder. I tasted the gall of betrayal, cruel laughter, unbridled rage. I tasted the sting of leather, the crack of flesh tearing open. I tasted a burden hefted through dusty streets, a breathlessness, the acrid tang of metal, despair, excruciating pain, thirst, the nausea of abandonment, and then.....

I almost choked. My whole body trembled at that final taste. I looked up at the old man in horror who was still smiling at me, sadly now. Was he a madman? Who would do such a thing?

"What do you taste, Leo?" the old man asked as dizziness overtook me.

I opened my mouth but no words came out. I couldn't answer.

"What do you taste?" he asked again.

I swooned and the world began to fade away. Distantly I felt the floor beneath me and a rush of people. Still that question screamed in my head.

What do you taste?

I tasted blood.

Over the next days everything tasted awful to me. No matter what I put in my mouth it all felt rotten and dying. It seemed I tasted blood everywhere.

Fresh vegetables were filled with rot, meat was spoiled, even wine had gone sour. I still had my same abilities, I knew the depth of all that I ate or drank. It was just that it all carried a taint. Everything that I put in my mouth was coated with a film that was the essence of decay. Or rather, I began to suspect it was me. My tongue had been fouled by disease and it putrefied everything that touched it.

Of course, I couldn't find the old man or his booth again. The Expo had no record of him or his company. I even took the floor manager to the very spot where the booth had been set up and he vehemently denied that there was any table there.

To make things worse my sleep was plagued with nightmares. I dreamt of every bad thing I had ever done in life. Every time I closed my eyes some old guilt bubbled up from deep within me, tortured me with memories of past regret.

I dreamt of the girls I seduced with no honest intentions. Too vividly did I remember my excitement in pursuing them and my eagerness to be away from them once they had given me what I sought.

The night played for me again how I had betrayed my college roommate, framing him for a wrong I had done. I saw again the people I belittled, the wineries I destroyed, the hurtful things I carelessly threw at others. Even the time in fourth grade when I hit Ronnie Sanders in the face with my lunch box rose up to plague my sleep. There wasn't a night that wasn't filled with guilt and grief. It was my life's worst moments lived over and over again.

For weeks this continued. During the day I could hardly eat or drink because my tastes had become corrupted. At night I couldn't sleep for dreams of sins past. I felt life draining from me, one day at a time. And for sure I would have died had things not changed.

It was Rome again, that same city where I had tasted the '45 Rothschild, I was hurrying from a nauseous meal back to my hotel. To even think of a nauseous meal in Rome seems heresy itself, but such was my curse. As I hurried through the city, not even taking in the majestic and ancient buildings I passed, I spied for an instant the old man from the Expo.

It was just a flash. For the briefest moment I caught the grey and grizzled beard, the deep set eyes. There was no mistaking that it was he who fed me that cursed wine.

Just barely did I catch him hurrying into an old church when the crowd closed in around me. I lost not a single second, barreling through the crowd and into the church.

The cold darkness of the church closed over me, lit only by the prayer candles that flickered in the narthex. A feeling of holy and silent dread filled me like the shadows behind the stained glass windows and the chilly glare of saints staring from the marble walls.

"Where are you?!" I screamed, not caring one whit about holy silence.

"I know you're here! Where are you?!"

"Peace, I am here," an old, velvety voice answered from the darkness beside me.

I whipped around to face the old man who looked at me with that same, sad smile. It was the same smile he wore as I lost consciousness at the Expo.

"What did you do to me? Who are you? What did you give me to drink?" I spit the questions out one on top of the other.

"What do you want to know first?" He asked back with his arms spread out.

"Who are you?"

"No one of consequence," he answered with a shrug. "An old priest with a dangerous curiosity. That is all."

"What did you give me to drink?" I questioned further. "What was that?"

"You are Leo the Incredible Wine Reader, are you not?" the old man smiled, broader this time. "What did you taste?"

My mouth turned dry and couldn't answer him. All of a sudden the whole thing seemed ridiculous to me. It couldn't be what I thought it was.

The old man only waited a moment for my answer and walked past me. He lit a prayer candle, quietly murmuring to himself and made the sign of the cross. I followed him into the sanctuary and stood beside the pew he seated himself in.

"What did you give me to drink?" I pressed insistently.

"A cheap merlot," the old man shrugged. "A seven dollar bottle out of California."

17

"No, there was more. You put something in it. Something awful."

"What did you taste?" the old man asked me again.

"I tasted blood," I whispered, barely able to gasp the words out.

The brows of the old man wrinkled up in thought. He smiled again and shook his head.

"The mysteries of God are difficult to ponder," he said. "Did you taste wine at all?"

"I did. At first I tasted your cheap merlot. Then I tasted a lot of other things: an old vintage, the Mediterranean air, crowds of people, suffering, betrayal, too much to mention. Then I tasted blood."

"It was communion wine," the old priest told me. "Wine but not wine. Blood but not blood."

A sudden sense of disorientation whirled through my head. I fell into the pew beside me before I fell down. The dark of the sanctuary seemed to come alive, to surround and fill me.

"What did I drink?" I just managed to ask. "What was it I tasted?"

"You tasted all that wine contained which no one else can taste," he told me. "You tasted suffering, you tasted love, you tasted a man paying the ultimate price for all that we have done wrong. You tasted the cross."

"Everything tastes awful to me now," I said. "I can't eat. I can't drink. There is a taint on me that fouls everything that goes into my mouth. I have awful dreams at night. Every second of the day I live in fear. Why? What did it do to me?"

The old priest leaned forward and folded his hands. A deep sigh rose from him as he looked up at the altar, his eyes steadily upon the crucifix hanging in frozen agony.

"You tasted sin," he said. "Now it won't leave you."

"Whose sin?" I asked.

"Your own," he chuckled, leaning back again to look me in the eye.

"You tasted your own sin and it taints everything in life. That's the nature of sin. It covers everything, touches everything, fouls everything."

Nothing the old priest said made any sense to me. How could I

18

taste my own sin in a glass of merlot? How did I taste blood? A thousand different questions stirred inside of me. But only one concerned me at the moment.

"How do I get rid of it?"

I stayed in the church all night. The old priest and I spoke at length. He told me things I had heard before but always ignored. Even hearing some of it for the first time it sounded familiar.

My whole life I always believed myself too sophisticated to believe as the masses believed. This whole business of being born again, accepting Jesus, repenting and the such was so plebeian I always turned my nose up at it. All that religious nonsense was for those who lacked refinement in life, who only had such superstitious habits to make their lowly lives worthwhile.

I see the truth now. All that refinement and sophistication that I believed made my life worthwhile only distracted me from the true meaning of life. Only after I saw my life for what it was, what it truly was, did I understand. All along I had used my snobbery as a shield, protecting me from the terror of living a deep life, protecting me from what I tasted in that glass of cheap, blessed merlot. I tasted the truth.

All that I was had been torn away with that one taste. Even as I spoke to the old man I cared nothing for his religion. Only I couldn't bear to live anymore as I was, not with that awful taint on everything. I even tried to resist further, leaving the church as the sun rose to mull things over for myself. One taste of breakfast brought it all back, the rot on everything that passed through my mouth.

That very day I was baptized and nothing has been the same since. Oh, there is much about me that is the same. I have my personality, my shortcomings, much in me that needs reform. But I am trying now. I am trying to be a better man.

My tastes I got back. The taint that had spilled over and infected everything was washed away as I was washed with baptism. I didn't taste the taint anymore, although from time to time I can detect hints. But I know now what I must do about it.

It was impossible to go back to my old life. I am no longer a food and wine critic. What is a critic anyway? Someone who stands on the sides and points out the flaws in the work of others. Easiest thing in the world to do, criticize, and a pretty cowardly way to live.

Now I work as a consultant to help improve food quality for any buyer, grower or purveyor of food and wine. My work now is to improve the finished product, not criticize it. I work so others can criticize.

I am still a food snob. With tastes like mine it is even more impossible to eat the antiseptic and plastic-tasting trash that fills our supermarkets and restaurants. But I am a different type of food snob.

My favorite foods are the simple ones now; an apple that holds all the taste of autumn, tomatoes full of summer goodness, carrots rich of the earth itself, a simple steak that carries in it the flavor of grass and open pasture. The food made by God is still the best.

Finally, I have found that wine I have searched for my whole life. Every Sunday I taste what has been missing, the piece that fills up the fullness of wine, the words for the blank pages in the book. You can scoff all you want, turn your nose up at me, but you can't taste like I can. You don't know what it's like to experience the true depth of the eucharist, the communion, when I gather with my greater family and we all partake together. I wish you could taste it too. It's the most beautiful thing I've tasted in my life.

It tastes like redemption.

Joseph Keysor
author of *Hitler, the Holocaust, and the Bible*

is proud to present the 2011

G.K. Chesterton Award

To

Kelly Rutland

Gladewater, TX

Second Place

(Category: 19 and up)

Bio:

Kelly is a graduate of Texas A&M University who enjoys writing scripts and short stories. His passion in life is cultural apologetics. He also has served in a jail ministry for over 10 years spreading the message of God's Grace. Kelly also enjoys golf, fishing and other outdoor activities.

He currently resides in Gladewater, TX with his wife Dana of fourteen years and two beautiful daughters Macy and Reese. They are expecting their third child this year.

THE VISIT

Kelly Rutland
All Rights Reserved

The baby blue 83' Caprice half slid into the driveway nearly clipping the trash can as it rest on top of the icy slush. The radio playing only out of the passenger door had Anne Murray singing:

*"Nobody robbed a liquor store on the lower part of town. Nobody
OD'ed, nobody burned a single buildin' down
Nobody fired a shot in anger, nobody had to die in vain
We sure could use a little good news today".*

Murray's soothing voice made it hard to turn the key off. But alas, it had to be done.

Just as she had suspected, the white two-story queen-anne style house was decked out for Christmas complete with a nativity scene in the yard that had once belonged to her mother. After a deep sigh and a glance at two old school pictures of her niece and nephew she kept taped to the dash of the old Caprice, she hesitantly grabbed the latch to open the door. The chrome handle was hot from the heater vent being directed at it the last two hours. It made her realize she was sweating.

How long had it been? Four, no five years she guessed. Her nephew Tanner had just started school the last time she had seen her sister. That was her best recollection anyway, so Millie was maybe a 2nd grader now. "Dinah, you must be the world's worst aunt." She muttered. "And sister." "God." She opened the door and the cold slapped her face, but it was soothed by the peaceful silence that can only be ushered in by a cleansing ivory snowfall. "The larger the flakes the better the scrubbing power" she thought. She believed she heard each individual flake touch down on her windshield like little fallen angels. Snows like that produce still moments in the soul that whisper "its okay" and demand a deep breath exhaled as a frosty offering to the clouds. The stillness is grand and the mind appreciates just being, not going or coming or planning or scheming. Just being and just being quiet. Dinah really missed the quiet soft things in life Flannel sheets, grandma's quilts… But, the sound of a passing car with tires smashing the dirty slush behind her on the street snapped her back to the worries of her life.

Dinah struggled to make her way along the slippery driveway to the side door by the garage. The feel of cold moisture on her sock from a weak spot in the sole of her boot aggravated her. She wondered if Annie had already spied her walking up. If so, was her sister weighing her options: open the door or pretend to hide? Each trepid step brought with it a new thought: "Could she even recognize me anyway?" and, "I wish I had some lipstick." And, "another new car under her perfectly organized garage" and, "why are we so different?" and, "Mom and dad would have been so proud" and finally- "here goes nothing". She stepped up and tapped on the door.

Surely, Anne was already dressed up ready to go to some luncheon though it was only 8am. "I know Princess Anne must be feeding the hungry and sheltering the homeless or something", she pictured her sister in the perfect tweed jacket and skirt. Pink no

22

less. "Baking cookies from scratch I bet and individually wrapping them for the Church ...what is taking so long Sis, its freezing out here." She grew aggravated from the cold and the thoughts - KNOCK KNOCK KNOCK!

Finally, the door gently opened. Dinah wasn't prepared to see her sister in a robe and no make-up. Did she wake her up? Still, she had the same beaming smile she recognized from when they were little after some discovery had been made which they thought was a major find. Anne could have just as easily been named Grace and not a soul would have been disappointed.

"Dinah! Dinah! Come in girl! Look at you! Where have you been? Praise God! Give me a hug! (big hug) Get in here!". "Give me your coat.", then another bigger hug that seemed it was going to squeeze the air out of Dinah's lungs just the way Mom would have done it.

Seeing Annie's eyes begin to well up, "Don't cry Annie, you are going to make me ball!" It was too late as both women had to dab at their eyes. "Where are the kids?"

"It's a school day Dinah. They won't be home until about three thirty or so." Dinah felt relieved and a bit foolish, but she had never had kids. She never dealt with things like school times, box lunches and birthday parties so they were foreign to her. On the other hand, Annie wouldn't know where to score any "speed", but it sure looked like she could use some right now.

"You got any coffee Anns? I got chilled on the stoop. What took you so long? I almost thought you weren't home." Annie was the name the family called her sister, Annette was what was on her birth certificate but Anns was what popped into Dinah's brain when she thought about "big sister". All at once a flood of Christmas memories of them sitting around a gaudy tree in their pajamas looking for boxes labeled "big sister" or "little sister" flowed through her mind. Those times seem but a prick of light down a long dark tunnel now. The years had dimmed so much of her memory of the best times of her life. Little flashes of such were a treat.

"Heavy cream and two sugars Di ?". Is that still how you take it? Annie had already moved to the counter. "Sit down at the table. We have a lot of catching up to do. You don't know what it means to me for you to be here - get comfortable. Are you hungry?", Annie was energized into big sister mode, all systems go, thrilled, best she had felt in a long time.

"Yes Anns. I still like it pa-paw style." She loved being able to say something so personal like that and it mean something to someone without explanation. "How is Mike doing? I guess he still has his firm?" She didn't really care about Mike that much. "What grade are the kids in now?"

"Mike will die at his desk, buried in one of those law books, and people won't even notice for two days. So yes he is still there. Tanner is in 5th grade now by the grace of God. That boy has your study habits I am afraid, but just like you he is smart as a whip, and Millie is doing fabulous in 7th. She is going to do a solo in a program this month for Christmas. I tell her she got that voice from her aunt Dinah. She looks like you and Tanner acts like you. He has your sense of humor. I see you in them and I see mom and dad of course."

Annie brought coffee and store bought cookies to the table. "No way! Store bought cookies? That's got to be some type of sin to Annette," Di mused to herself. "Surely Annie must have not been able to afford time away from crafts or scrap booking in order to justify store bought cookies! Wow, I guess one of the stars fell off of Wonder Woman's panties" she continued to joke inside herself.

The women chatted like girls and the time passed easily. Dinah saw softness from Annie and she did not get the usual questions that always came around that could be such a buzz kill. It had been a long time since a visit went without the feel of the Great White Throne Judgment. Instead of critique, Annie discussed vacations taken, activities the kids were in, Mike's accomplishments, what her church was involved in, but not much about herself. Dinah volunteered the minimum. Yes, she had a boyfriend. The same one Annie didn't much care for, though they had never met. She had traveled and lived in various cities with Jason. No, she no longer sang and played, having sold her guitar a few years back. "Marriage? Not for me." She interjected. Don't want to, of course. Still, she made glance at her own barren ring finger.

Two hours in, no cookies left and no inquiries yet about her "using" and relationship reprimands about "living in sin" or "don't you want children?" As Annie was reminding her about some long ago adventure they shared in high school, she noticed past the big smile and high cheeks that her sister had gotten older. That twinkle from her eye that won over everybody she met (especially men) was somehow dimmer. Her hair so short now, made Dinah want to tell her it looked a little butch, but Anns had just been too sweet to this point to pull the trigger on that. Still she would keep that bullet chambered. Anns looked tired and regardless of how different they were, Dinah loved her. Was the Junior League poisoning her body as well as her mind? Dinah always suspected so.

"Annie, what about you?" Dinah broke in. "You have told me everything about everyone, but not about you. What kind of fundraiser are you heading up? Aren't you and Mike renewing your vows or something edifying like that?" She did not intend for it to sound so mean, but it did, and she caught a glimpse of hurt in Annie's eyes. She regretted it. "I mean what is going on with you, my big sister that I love so much?"

"Well, I am doing okay. I don't do much outside activities anymore really. I do stuff for the kids, you know, class parties, bake sales and stuff like that. I am still tending to the flower beds at church and occasionally work in the kitchen at the mission. Mostly, I have just been a mom and wife. Mike and I are doing great. I don't know what I would do without him. We have been blessed for sure. We sometimes wish we would have started having kids sooner. We didn't realize what a blessing they would be to our lives. I do wish you were around them more Di. I wish they could get to know you, know us, you know?" Dinah knew Annie really meant that. She regretted not spending time with her and her kids, but how could she? She we damaged goods.

"You know I can't do that, Annie. Mike wouldn't stand for it and he would be right. I wouldn't respect him if he did. They don't need me in their lives. I would rather you just let them know the best part of me. I want to them to think of me like that picture you have of me in the hall by the bathroom. I was happy then, respectable, you know? Clean." Unconsciously she ran her tongue across her front teeth that no longer shined like they did when that picture was taken. She felt ashamed she had let that happen. "I need to smoke." Dinah abruptly stood up and moved to her coat hanging next to the door, and jumbled her hands in the big pockets looking for the lighter and the familiar feel of cellophane. Finally, she desperately squeezed her hand onto the empty pack. She is out, "Unfreakin believable." She could have sworn she had one left. "Always when you need it the most!" she thought.

"Di you don't have to go outside. It's too cold, just smoke in here." Annie was concerned for her sister, but really she did not want to miss out on a moment with her.

Dinah laughed, "Ohhh, no. Mike will have a fit if he gets even the slightest hint that someone has broached his castle with a smoke. I was worried about dropping an ash off the porch!"

"Don't worry about Mike. Just stay with me and smoke here." pleaded Annie.

"It's okay. I am alright, just a stupid habit. I don't need to smoke anyway. I have been cutting way back. Really, I …"

"You are wrong, by the way. They do need you in their life. You have a lot to offer them. There is more to you than just mistakes that you have made. I think the kids would see so much of themselves in you with your wit and talent. They also can get a better idea of Mom and Dad, you know? I mean they can only get so much of what Mom and Dad were like from me. You look so much like Mom and act so much like Dad and I just - Dinah, I just need you, too. You know, I miss you. I want to see your face, but even a phone call would be ... you know. I just don't understand why you don't want to be near us, near me.

Dinah had to look away. She couldn't stand to see her sister cry, but how could Annette understand what its like to live, to *have* to live, with such dissatisfaction. Has she ever wanted to disappear, to not be, to not breathe regret as a way of life? She has always been so satisfied and grateful for everything... and why wouldn't she be? Look how lucky she is in her spotless little world with her spotless things in her spotless house with her spotless brain. Where is her darkness? What's in the crevices of her closet that want to crawl out and play? "Why do you want me here? We are nothing alike! I smoke, I drink, I curse, and I do drugs. God knows I do drugs, and all your Nancy Reagan friends can't deal with that! All I have to do is "JUST SAY NO", and I won't, so I must be demon possessed. Not everyone is happy on this crappy rock we live on like you are, not everyone likes the music being played and your type can't understand that. I want to pick my own music to dance to. Most of the people you know would not even sit at the table with me if they were here with us now. Why would I want to be around that?

"That's not true." Annie attempted but Dinah rolled her eyes and neck. "Well it's mostly not true. Look Dinah, you can condemn my friends all you want but c'mon you scare them. You scare me! That lifestyle scares me! Your nefarious drug friends and all that business, I mean you know people who at least know people who would kill somebody for a little cash. I worry about you all the time. I just wish"-she stopped herself short.

"I scare you, but you want me to be around you and the kids? Oh okay, I am supposed to come along, but I won't bring any of my tattooed, pierced, drinking, drugging, devil worshiping friends with me? Lord forbid I might bring Jason! I will forget I love him, so you and I can spend some Saturdays when you're not busy, of course, and we can scrap book! I mean really Annette, you live up here in your ivory tower with your matching Escalades, Waterford crystal, and custom marble floors" Dinah searched for one more item. There it is, "... and built in refrigerator and I am trying to figure out how to get an inspection sticker on my car not to mention gas to get back home! I mean really, you don't know what its like to do without, not for a long time. You want me, but in your place, at your time and on your terms. You don't want ME you want your version of me! You're just like all the other church people!" Dinah had not intended to bring that tirade. This was not the plan. She told herself not to go there, but isn't this what always happens? Shoot the lights and curse the dark. "You just want me to make you feel better about me."

Annette didn't put up much of a fight, but she came with what she had, "and you just want money."

Dinah took the type of deep breath one takes when confronted by a truth, but not whole truth, "Not just money. I'm just saying-

Annie jumped back in, "Where is your place Di? What is your address? Where do I come to? What number do I call to set something up? Where do you go? Where do you sleep? Who of your friends do I need to know? Where are you Dinah? Where do I find you? How do I come to meet your terms?"

Dinah deflected, "It's always 'come to church, come to bible study' or something. Did you ever think for one moment that maybe I would like to share a beer with my sister? Would it have hurt you to come to my ground a little? Why does everything with you have to have a sanctimonious bow wrapped around it?

"Nothing." Annie bowed her head.

"What's nothing" asked Dinah confused.

Nothing. It would have hurt nothing for me to have had a beer with you. I wished I had. I'm sorry. It never crossed my mind. I wished we would have done many things. And it's true, everything I do, everything I see or have, I associate with God. Or maybe I see it through Christ filtered glasses. I can't help that Di. I don't want to change that. It's who I am Dinah, just as much as I am your sister. Just as much as you are who you say you are." She wondered if she had really been that preachy all these years. Really? Annie charged, "Seriously, when did you ever *actually* come to bible study, or church or baptism or anything that I have ever asked you to come to? If you had asked me to have a beer with you with the passion you just showed now, I would like to think I would have said yes. Ask yourself this. How much more do you think I cared to have you, my sister, see Millie baptized?"

"Look, I am sorry. I will just go" Dinah approached for a good-bye hug, but really she just wanted to make amends and flee.

"You know Dinah, I don't remember you asking me to come with you anywhere, or do anything? I don't remember all this rejection that I have heaped upon you. I do remember crying in the bed at night wondering where you were, hoping you would call. Wishing I could come get you. How many times have I wanted to pick you up in my arms like my baby sister? But you didn't. You won't have me near you. You *must* hate me, and for what? Because I have things; you would let good things in my life separate us? I just don't understand how you have come to hate me."

Dinah did not know what to say. She didn't hate her sister per se. She just hated. She just hated everything and nothing at the same time. Did she love Jason? Does he love her? What does love even look like? Does it matter? She didn't know anymore. Why the angst? Tortured she threw out a bomb, "Mom had an abortion, you know." She stared ahead at the target awaiting the destruction to amass.

"I've known that, Sis." Annie disarmed Dinah's revelation.

"Yeah? I didn't know you knew. I thought it was just something between mom and me." Dinah felt a twisted sense of betrayal. "Well, doesn't it bother you that we are supposed to have a big brother or sister or something? Don't you wonder what those dynamics would have been like? Especially, with an older brother?"

"I've wondered a lot of times. Would he have been like Dad?" She traced the rim of her coffee cup with her finger, "Would he have looked after us after, you know, after the accident and been the "man of the house". It would have been nice. An older sister would have been nice, too. But what does that have to do with you, Dinah? Blame me if you want, but don't blame mom-"

"Me too. I should be a mom, Annie. I just couldn't see how…" Dinah bit her lip.

Annie sat down in the kitchen chair holding her side. She put her head down on the table without saying a word. Dinah stared at her sister until she realized that Annie was weeping.

"Look, I am just gonna go. Anns, I do love you. Always have. Always will." Dinah regretted everything. "I shouldn't have told you. I shouldn't have come here. It doesn't concern you."

Annie raised herself up, "Why would you do that? Why didn't you come to me? If you didn't want the child, I would have gladly raised and loved your baby!"

Dinah said, "It doesn't involve you Annie! It was my body, it was inside me, it would have been wrong of me to bring a baby into… it wasn't a child yet anyway." It was my right and I did what was best for everyone."

Annie shot back, "What right do you have to rob me of my nephew or niece?" She slammed her hands on the table shaking it and shot up to her feet, "What right did Mom have to rob us of an older brother or sister? Did she not think that maybe I would have liked to have had someone there for me in my times of trouble? I might need someone that I could look in their face and see the eyes of my father or the smile of my mother. Someone I could seek out for counsel, someone to pick me up and encourage me and to go to when I am scared! Dinah, what gives you the right? It's not just your body and just your life. It's just not." She gathered her breath and cut Dinah off, "I want my kids to have cousins, to have someone to get together with at Thanksgiving and Christmas, someone in whom they can see my face when I am gone. I want them to know you Dinah, they need to know you. Don't let your feelings for me keep you from loving my children. You are all I have for them; all that has some of me anyway. Don't take that from them."

Dinah dropped her coat and raised her eyes upward, "It's not you, Annie. It's me! I am damaged! No one needs me, especially your children for God's sake! What really matters anyway? What is there about this life that really matters? I understand- you got kids. Even they will grow up and do their own thing and have their own lives. What is the point of all this stupid life- all this misery? Don't you get sick of having to wake up and do it all over again, this miserable little game? And what is worse, you don't get to set the rules and the rules in play are all stacked against you. I'm not like you, Annie. I question. I RAGE! I just wish you would shake your fist or something, for Christ's sake."

Annie reached for strength, dried her eyes and returned volley, "How arrogant, Dinah. You see me as this little silly ignorant girl that doesn't know better. You are so much deeper than your Pollyanna big sister. You have the world's angst on your shoulders and what are you to do? Let me tell you, just because I have faith does not mean I don't have questions. I don't turn a blind eye just because I think God will do right by me. I know suffering too. Cars and goblets and jewelry aren't my salve for how I hurt. They would not solve your problems either. I don't turn toward things. I turn to Christ and He gives me peace and for that you think I'm stupid. You turn to pills, but I should respect your existentialist nonsense as brilliance? Do you remember Ecclesiastes?

"For with much wisdom comes much sorrow;

the more knowledge, the more grief."

There is nothing new under the sun Dinah and that includes your self-analysis and social commentary and meaningless view of the world. You're right though, life is meaningless the way you live it. No God- No Meaning- No Purpose- No life. Am I supposed to applaud you for that? But never mind with that. I won't dare bother you with Christ, nor dare judge. You point your finger everywhere at everyone, but we are silly fools with our silly lives. If that is the case, I guess I am the problem!

Dinah dropped her face, "I said it's not you, Annie! It's me! I am the one covered in all this ...all this filth! Not you! No, not you, it's me! Repenting is easy when it's about a white lie or whatever someone like you might feel guilty about. My issues are just a little deeper than begging off a PTA meeting Sis. And you want me to just let your Savior wrap his arms around me?! What kind of God would do that?! Huh? I don't want to be that type of hypocrite. I am past change. I am who I am. C'mon Annie, it's easy for you to believe. Look at you, look around you. Where has He shown His face to me? Where is my sign? Huh? You've never done things you're ashamed of just so you could make some money for you and your knight in shining armor to get by on. You've never had a dark stranger tug at you every minute. You've never supported that habit. You've never..." she had to stop short. She could not go further with her confession or else the pain might be too much. Still shameful moments flashed through her mind's eye, frame by dirty frame, reminding her of how she had fallen. "I hate myself Annie!!! I wish I never was. I wish I never was!" Dinah crumpled to her knees and just sobbed. Annie knelt beside her little sister, putting her cheek into those curls that had defined Di's face since she was little.

"Baby girl, you just need to (she wanted to fix things but then said the only thing she could say) ...seek Him. Remember what we were taught Di, He did not come into the world to condemn, but to save." She whispered softly making prayerful pauses as if floating petitions on high. "Come just as you are and knock on His door. He loves you, Di, just as you are. Look back for Him, He is there, always has been. I promise He is good." She continued her whisper, her hope. "That is why it is called the Good News. The Gospel means good news! Don't you see Dinah; it is precisely because we are covered by this filth that God came in the flesh. He wants to save us from sin, to save us from ourselves. Annie continued softly, "Don't you see? Dinah He loves you, even now, especially now, He loves you and me– that is the good news. That is very good news indeed. He has paid for all of this grime, disease and death and one day soon, there will be none of it". Annie's voice tailed off and they both softly sobbed in each other's arms on the kitchen floor.

"I miss Him Anns, I really do. I just don't love Him anymore" she sobbed harder.

She tried to quell her little sister's sobs like so many times before, but instead of a knee, this was her heart that was skinned,

"Shhhhhh… its okay… Di- He still loves you… He is faithful… You will see…. Trust me… Trust Him… He will never leave you nor forsake you… In His time Sis, when you turn around you will bump into him…

He will be there… I promise."

After a very long moment, another knock came to the door and it opened before being answered. A young woman peeked in, "Annette?" The lady glanced down as Dinah and Annie stirred back to their feet. "Good Lord, Ms. Annette, are you okay? Is she fine? Are you fine?" her face darted back and forth between the sisters seeking an answer.

"I am fine, Claire. I'm fine. Just tired." Claire helped Annette to her feet. " I think I will lie down. Dinah make your self at home, please stay for dinner and see the kids when they get off the bus. I want to talk some more, okay?" Claire coaxed Annette out of the kitchen and down the hall.

"Who is that?" Dinah asked herself. "Annie, are you okay?" she half yelled? "Whew, I am tired too." she sniffled and glanced at the clock on wall and realized she had to be going. This visit was not exactly what she was wanting, but she was still glad it happened. Claire walked back in with a manila envelope.

"Annette asked me to give you this in case you couldn't stay." She handed it off. "Are you a friend or family?"

Dinah read the front of the envelope with her name hand written on it, "Annie and I went to school together." Dinah lied to avoid any probing conversation. "And you are?"

"We go to church together; I have been helping out when I can. I am glad you got to see her. Maybe you can come back soon? She gets tired so quickly now."

The blood drained from Dinah's face at those familiar words, her heart failed and her fingers went cold, "Oh Lord. What do you mean- tired now?"

"I mean she is just so much weaker from when she was diagnosed a year and a half ago. She is a fighter though, making it this long. I know she has put up such a good fight for those poor kids of hers. She does love them so."

Dinah made a step to the hall and then quickly back to the door snatching her coat. She wanted to run to her sister, but instead, "I have to leave. Nice meeting you… uhmm"

"Claire."

"Nice meeting you, Claire. Please take good care of her. I have to go now." Dinah could barely get her mouth to work properly. She was ensconced in fear or shame or both. Out the door, she wanted to sprint through the snow, but it felt like a trudge. Still, she got to the car quickly and turned the key. Before she could straighten the car out on the street and put it into drive she was overwhelmed by her grief, her desperate love for her sister and still more tears poured down her face. She groaned in despair over the sound of methodical wipers swiping back and forth over ice and snow. She wailed and her groans rose from deep inside her. She continued this way for blocks until the first stop light forced her into composure.

Dinah checked the rearview and threw out a prayer, "God, I am such a mess." She pushed in the cigarette lighter and then remembered she had no more cigarettes. In frustration she pulled it out again and threw the igniter at the passenger window. She gnashed her teeth to hold back the suffering that wanted to erupt from that place deep inside her. This was a place that scared her because of its torrential pain and despair. She knew it twice before, because those depths had been dredged before when her parents had died. The lighter had tumbled onto the seat next to the manila envelope. The outside read "To my Di" in beautiful cursive. Dinah picked it up and unwound the little string which held down the flap and pulled out five crisp one-hundred dollar bills and another document with the heading "Providential Life Insurance Company". Further down it read "sole beneficiary Ms. Dinah Stinson" and just over from that "Sum of 2,000,000.00" Finally, a yellow sticky note that read, "Mike make sure to keep this safe for Dinah. She will come back. Make sure she gets this. I believe in her". Through swollen eyes Dinah scoped the inside of the envelope a second time and spied a crisply folded piece of paper that had been torn from a spiral note book. The ragged edge of the paper did not want to let go of its resting spot, but Dinah fingered it out and unfolded it to read:

Dinah, if you are reading this, then I have left this world. I want you to know I love you. I love you SO MUCH. I know we have had differences, but I only remember the times when we have been best of friends. I think back to us playing dolls, riding bikes, sitting at the Dairy Cream and talking about boys that drove by. Do you remember sharing our fears and our hopes? Do you remember all the laughing we did? Please remember that Di. Death has made me prioritize my life and make an assessment of my time here on earth. Please forgive me sister for the times that I did not listen, or try to understand you. Please forgive me for not expressing to you how much you mean to me and that includes those things that make us different. I don't know how I allowed us to get away from each other. I regret that. I should have done more. I am sorry I haven't been there for you as I should have. Deep inside, I have never wanted you to be another version of me. I have never needed that. But, I suppose I have pushed you to be like me just so I wouldn't have to see you in such pain. I wanted to fix you. That is selfish of me and I truly regret it. Now I only wish I would have just spent more time in your presence. I love you for who you are, my sister, and would not have you any other way. I believe in you Di. I knew you would come back to me. I also know that you will get past your troubles and that you are strong just like mom and dad.

I hope that when you read this, things have turned for the best for you. However, if they haven't you should still count yourself rich. Your troubles are not the end of the story, those marks on your arms don't define you. Jesus said, "Blessed are the poor in spirit for theirs is the Kingdom of Heaven." The good news Dinah is that in our weakest moments, when we have nothing to offer, is when we can hear the Good Shepherd calling. God accepts us and loves and wishes us to come to Him just as we are. He will then do a good work in you. That is the Good News indeed! Call out to Him. Slip His ring on your finger. If you are in one of those moments, call out to Him my sister and take a bite. You will see that God is good.

The next time we see each other, it will be forever!

Love my Children for me,

Annie

Traffic had stacked up behind her as she sat motionless before the green light of the intersection. The frustrating honks did not move her and cars and trucks began to pass her by. She threw the gear shift in park and let off the brake. Dinah stirred around in her purse trying to find her cell phone. Hastily she decided to just dump it out upside down in the seat. Finally, she grabbed the phone and began punching numbers. The light changed again, the wipers swiped and swooshed, more cars honked but Dinah did not move. Tears streaked down her face as she was holding the phone with her shoulder, and the money in one hand and the tear stained letter in the other. Ring after ring went by as her eyes roamed from one hand to the other. She knew at this intersection a decision must be made. Her life's direction would be made in this moment, at this icy juncture in the next few billowy breaths. Her heart pounded in her throat as she anticipated the defining moment for when her call would be answered. Ring after sickening ring went by. The wiper blades also chorused this final countdown like circling hyenas....

until finally a voice on the other end answered. Dinah could barely make her voice work, as so often happens after true sorrow has welled up from ones guts. Her lungs were making her body jerk as they attempted to resolve the pain she was feeling. She tried to catch her breath, then like a child she softly answered back, "Jason, it's me... Yes, I did and I am on my way back. I have to tell you something. Jason, babe, I've got..." she caught herself looking at the taped pictures on the dash and was crying again having made her choice "I've got good news."

ChristianManuscriptSubmission

is proud to present the 2011

George MacDonald Award

To

Richard Gibson

Maplewood, MO

Third Place

(Category: 19 and up)

Bio:

Richard Louis Gibson is 22-years old and lives in Maplewood, Missouri. He can't decide about college or about a day job or about most other major decisions in his life, but he is decided about at least three things: He loves YHWH, he loves his wife, and he loves writing.

Jude

Richard Gibson

The last day of school before Christmas break always made everyone a little extra raucous. High schoolers in a somewhat-small town are rowdy anyway because of their boredom, but the added excitement of both Christmas and Christmas break only served to increase it.

And that made eavesdropping so much more fun.

"This is the kid, isn't it?" I heard a guy say behind me.

"Yep," his friend replied. "The kid with the jackets."

"What's his name again?"

"'Judah', but he goes by 'Jude'."

Eavesdropping isn't as much fun when you know who and what is being talked about, so I kept walking. I could hear that their voices grew quiet and their footsteps drew closer. They were getting as near as they figured they could without being heard over the din of the student body exiting the school building. They kept a good proximity, too far for me to hear their breathing, but close enough to examine me.

"Wow, look at this thing," the first one said.

"Seriously, dude," the friend responded. I recognized his voice as someone in my grade. "It is as cool as they say."

I smiled broadly. I loved hearing that. It was basically the best compliment I had ever received, and I heard it maybe every other week. Sure, it was a compliment about my jacket, not directly about me, but it was a compliment about my handiwork, so that's a good enough compliment for an artist. Since this was the only senior high school in town, and therefore rather large, it took a while for word to get around. As such, my jackets were still essentially folklore.

"Think he'd make me one?" the one in my grade asked.

I stopped and spun around, almost causing them to run into me. I immediately realized that he was one of the "popular" kids. What a joke. I held up a hand and wagged my finger. "Not a chance, buddy."

His surprise quickly changed to sadness, then even more quickly to disdain. "Why not? I'll hook you up with some gorgeous chicks in exchange."

I laughed and shook my head. "No, you're not getting one. This isn't a label or a brand name. These are one-of-a-kind pieces of signature artwork." I could see he was rather angry, so I persisted. "And, they're mine." With that, I spun on my heel and walked off.

#

Once outside the building, I sprinted towards David's monstrous pick-up truck and jumped into the bed of it.

As soon as my heavy shoes hit the metal, he yelled, "Jude! Get in here! We don't got time to waste!"

Thomas chimed in. "Yeah yeah, get in here."

I laughed and got in the truck's cab. "What's the rush?"

"We're running down to Stonewall's," Thomas said as he moved between David and me and buckled himself in.

"Jackson's Junction?" I asked as I too buckled my seatbelt.

"No, we're going to see a wall of rocks. Of course!" He quickly drove off the school parking lot, weaving in and out of cars, and flooring it as soon as he was on the main road. There was a reason both Thomas and I wore our seatbelts, and it had nothing to do with the law.

I put my backpack on the floor and said, "Assuming we make it there alive, what're we going there for?"

David simply glared at me. "You just fulla questions, aren't ya?"

I nodded. "You guys been saving your money?"

"No, we've spent it all on flowers and candy. Of course we have!" David said.

"Yeah yeah, we've been saving it," Thomas said.

"Well, good," I said. "I bet we'll have enough after Christmas, so long as my parents don't spoil my kid twin brothers again."

#

"Jackson's Junction" is pretty slow during the winter, what with it being an outdoor carnival-like place. However, the indoor go-kart track was open year-round, and there were two special attractions right now: For starters, there was a brand-new track, one that was only available to skilled drivers. All three of us qualified, but that may have just been because we had gotten on the good side of Phillip Jackson, the owner.

In addition to that, he had just bought a slew of brand-new, high-end go-karts and replaced all the older ones. He wasn't going to let anyone use them until after Christmas, but we wanted to see if he'd let us, anyway, so we would be the first ones to drive them.

While driving new karts on a new track was basically the coolest thing ever, that wasn't the real reason we were going. Not entirely. We wanted to see if he still had any of the older model go-karts available for sale. Mr. Jackson wasn't one to throw things away, especially not when he could make a buck off of them. He had sold the rest of the karts to other track owners in other states, but he said he'd hold three of them for a while for us, but only if we could pay for all three at once and up front, that is.

It was really a shame that my parents wouldn't let me buy one, so I had to earn and save the money behind their backs. I figured once I bought it, though, Mr. Jackson wouldn't take it back, so they'd have to let me keep it. Besides, maybe they'd be impressed that I actually worked for and saved my own money.

Once we got to Jackson's Junction, Mr. Jackson wouldn't even talk to us about them. "I told ya'll ya can't have 'em until ya got the money for 'em!"

"But you haven't even told us how much they are," I said.

"Yeah yeah, you haven't," Thomas said.

Mr. Jackson narrowed his eyes. "Ya don't have enough, trust me."

"Mr. Jackson, you don't even know how much money we have," I said.

"It's not enough, now off with ya!" he bellowed.

Yes, this is considered being on his good side.

We did as he demanded and drove off. David was the first to speak. "What an ass!"

"Yeah yeah, a real jerk," Thomas concurred.

"Hey now," I said. "He's probably right. We gotta make some more money and hope our parents give us some real cash for Christmas. There's no other way we'll have enough."

"That only gives us three working days," Thomas said.

"Better make 'em count." David said, and that was that.

#

Those three working days passed without event and without any sort of income, but that didn't matter. Now the big day had finally arrived: December 25th, Christmas day.

"Merry Christmas, Judah!" my parents yelled too loudly as they handed me my final box. It was my last present of the year.

It had better be good, I thought as I took it from their hands and glanced behind me at my paltry assortment of gifts, then to my side at my kid brothers' overflowing piles. This last box was about two feet long, a foot wide, a few inches deep, and rather light. *Clothes.* I smiled at them. "Thanks, guys."

I opened it quickly, anyway. Opening a present is exciting, even if you're entirely positive that it's only clothes and nothing more.

"It's a shirt!" I said as I lifted the lid.

My twin brothers laughed, but a look from me saying, "That's not cool," was all it took to shut them up.

My father tilted his head from behind the video camera. "No, it isn't."

"Take it out!" my mother cried. "Take it out!"

"Okay, okay." I did so, and I realized it was a jacket. "Oh, it's a jacket."

"Do you like it?!" My mother was basically hopping. "Do you like it!?"

Dad shook his head. "Dear, let him look at it first."

"Yeah, Mom," I said. I held it up.

First off, let me just say that it was all wrong. It had that stupid, clearly-trendy-big-brand pre-ripped look. It had a thick hood, skulls drawn on it, a huge zipper, only one small pocket, and the thumb holes were in the wrong spot and not reinforced or padded. To top it off, it was thin and cheap-looking. The only thing it was missing was a huge garish label.

In addition to all of this, all the tags were gone and it smelled like the detergent Mom used.

I looked at them. "Did you--"

"We actually did all of that ourselves!" Mom squealed.

"I may as well have been cutting myself with that razor," Dad added.

"Honey!" she scolded.

I was speechless. "Wow. It's... uh--"

"We knew you'd like it!" Mom turned to Dad. "See? I told you he'd love it."

"Yes, dear," he replied. Even though I couldn't see his face, I knew he rolled his eyes.

I tried to smile. "Thanks," I said. I put it back in the box, but before I could close the lid, Mom spoke.

"Well, put it on, Jude!"

"Don't you need to wash it first?" I asked.

She was more excited than I could understand. "We already did! It's all ready for you to wear!"

"Oh..."

"Put it on! Put it on!"

"Dear," Dad said. "He's already wearing a jacket."

39

"Yeah, so, this one's new. Besides, <u>dear</u>," she said, glaring at Dad. "he <u>needs</u> to put it on."

"Oh, yeah," he said, looking thoughtful.

She looked like she might flip her lid. "Come on, Jude!"

But I didn't want the thing touching my skin if I could avoid it, so I changed the subject: I reached behind me and grabbed a box. "Here, Dad, this is for you."

He was taken aback. "What? Really?"

Mom turned on a dime. "Don't act so surprised, honey. You know we all love you."

"Here," I said. "I'll take the camera. Open it!"

He laughed as he traded me the camera for the present. "It better not be a tie!"

The rest of Christmas day was uneventful and standard. My brothers both got not only exactly what they wanted and then some, but about twice as much as I did. I wasn't surprised or hurt, though, because it happened every year. Well, maybe a little hurt.

#

The next day, David and Thomas met at my place. We had decided even before Christmas break that we would meet at my house on the 26th to talk to Mr. Jackson again. We figured that our Christmas cash plus the Christmas spirit together would encourage Mr. Jackson to sell us the go-karts.

But I didn't even get out the door before my plans began to go awry. I did my usual call-as-I'm-walking-out-the-door routine. "Mom! I'm going to hang out with David and Thomas! I'll be back before dinner!"

"Ok!" she called back. "Oh, wait! Jude!"

I stopped with my hand on the knob. Something about her tone didn't bode well.

She appeared at the end of the hallway with a garment in her hand. "Why don't you wear your new jacket?" She tossed it to me.

I was already wearing one, but I caught it and nodded. "Thanks, Mom."

"Well, then you won't need that one you're wearing, will you?"

What is her deal with this crummy jacket?! I hesitated. "Thomas usually gets cold." I didn't lie; I just didn't tell the whole truth.

She smiled. "Well, that would be nice to share your jacket with him." She turned away, but then back to me. "But, uh, just... make sure you wear that one, ok?" She pointed to the one she just tossed me, the new one she made for me, the awful one, the branded one.

Everyone else in the world knows I'd never let anyone else wear one of my signature jackets. But, as usual, my mother knew nothing about me. I was really starting to understand the whole teen-angst thing. "Sure thing, Mom. Bye!" I ran out the door before anything else bad could happen.

David and Thomas were already waiting at the curb.

"What took ya?" David asked.

"Aliens," I said as I opened the door and climbed into the cab.

Thomas moved to the middle, as usual, and laughed. "The female parental unit, huh?"

"What else?"

He pointed at my new jacket. "What's that?"

"It's nothing, trust me," I replied as I threw it onto the dashboard.

David noted it, but refrained from saying anything. Thomas, as usual, did not. "Since when were you into labels?"

I glared at him. "You're kidding, right?"

David said, "Shut it up and let's go!"

"Yeah yeah, let's do this!" Thomas yelled.

No sooner had I shut the door than David was going fifty miles per hour, making a nigh two-wheeled turn out of my subdivision.

"Assuming we get there alive," I said. "do you guys think we'll have enough cash?"

David said nothing, and Thomas's tone didn't bode well. "I didn't get any Christmas cash, not even from any relatives. They all sent gift cards."

David roared, "Just a bunch of damn gift cards!"

His anger silenced us and got us to Jackson's Junction in record time. When we burst in the door, Mr. Jackson turned on us with a glare that would have killed a normal man, but he brightened and relaxed when he saw it was just us.

"What do you hoodlums want?" he bellowed.

Thomas spoke first. "Do you still have those go-karts for us?!"

"I said I'd hold 'em 'til the end of the year."

"You never put a time limit on it," I said.

Thomas spoke up. "Yeah yeah, nor did you tell us how much they were."

Mr. Jackson waved a hand. "I never told ya how much they were because you kids probably can't make that much," he shrugged. "Do you want me to get your hopes up and then break your fool hearts?"

"Well, is this enough?" Thomas asked, pulling out his wallet.

David and I followed his actions. We each pulled out all of our cash and spread it out on the counter so Jackson could see it. I noticed that Thomas and David each had about thirty dollars more than I did. Apparently I was more extravagant and had squandered more than I thought, though my parents were also stingier than theirs.

Mr. Jackson's eyes widened a very small amount upon seeing all the green paper in front of him. Though it was a small reaction, we knew he was flabbergasted.

He glanced at it all, counting in his head, I suppose. Suddenly, he grew almost angry. "I told ya it was all or nothin'! I won't have ya fighting over who gets them when. If ya can't pay for all three of 'em, ya don't get any of 'em!" With that, he turned and went into his office, almost slamming the door shut.

David turned on me. "Dammit, Jude!"

"Yeah yeah, man, what gives?" Thomas added.

I shrugged, pocketing my cash. "Yeah, well, if my parents hadn't spoiled my kid brothers so much, I'd have enough."

"Or if you hadn't tried to bribe Madeline into being your girlfriend!" Thomas said.

I glared at him. "Hey, now, that's not--"

"Let's go!" David yelled. "We gotta get you some money, quick!"

We raced to his car and he sped off almost faster than he had driven here.

#

In a somewhat-small town like ours where nearly everybody knows you, it's easy to make a little cash doing next to nothing. At least for the retail stores in the mall on the south side, the day after Christmas was almost worse than Black Friday in terms of heavy traffic, but it was definitely worse in terms of sales. Instead of purchasing, everybody was doing returns or, at best, exchanges.

For kids like us, though, both days were the same: a time to help little (or large) old (or ancient!) ladies carry their packages to and from their cars. David, Thomas, and I had been doing this for years, so we knew which women were more likely to pay and, as such, we only talked to them. This isn't charity work, mind you.

Luckily for us, Miss Martin was pulling up just as we arrived. I leapt from David's truck to her car and put on the charmer's mask. "Hello, Miss Martin! Do you need any help with your packages today?"

She laughed. "Did you know I was coming or what? Of course I do!" She opened the door and handed me three bags and took one herself. All were larger than normal, filled with name brand junk. "My spoiled brat grandkids are so damn hard to please!" She covered her mouth. "Excuse me, it's just--"

I shook my head and said, "I understand, Miss Martin. Kids these days." People like her typically love that line.

She patted my head and ate the line like it was saltwater taffy. "But you're different, aren't you, Jude?"

After about an hour of being her little slave, she handed me a good old Alexander Hamilton. "Thank you, Jude, for being the future of our country," she said as she pinched my cheek.

Gag me. I quickly but gently took the bill and said, "Think nothing of it, Miss Martin. Have a good day." I even opened and closed her door for her. It's good customer service.

David and Thomas met me at the door to the mall. "How much more do you need, slacker?" David asked.

"About twenty will make me equal with you guys."

They handed me roughly a buck eighty in loose change, and Thomas said, "I assume she paid you more than this."

"Of course. Would I work for less?"

David spoke. "No, but we still need more. Come on!"

We scrounged the mall but didn't find any of the usual patsies and only a few quarters in change, so I figured we needed a new plan.

"Perhaps something more honest?" Thomas suggested as we left the mall.

I shook my head and, as I did, something caught my eye. Our winters aren't unbearably cold, but one needs at least a jacket, especially to stay out long in the cold. So, when I saw that obviously homeless man shivering, I knew he had been out in the open for some time, because his coat, though it looked like moldy Swiss cheese, was rather thick.

"Hold on, guys," I said. "I got an idea."

"What is it?" David asked.

"Unlock your truck, quick, come on."

He did so with the remote. "What's the rush? We got time, Jude."

I grabbed my new jacket and ran over to the man.

"Oh, no. This won't end well," David said as he saw what I was doing.

"Yeah yeah, this is bad," Thomas said.

#

"Sir?" I said as I approached the homeless man.

He turned to me, rather startled. He glanced around and realized I had to be talking to him. "Why are you calling me 'sir'?" His voice was much steadier than I thought it would be, considering the shivering and all.

"Would you like this jacket, sir?" I raised the jacket so he could see it.

He looked as if he might cry. "You would <u>give</u> that to a man like me?"

"Well, no, actually." I rubbed the back of my neck. I didn't think this would be quite so uncomfortable. "You see, I'm in need of some money. Do you have ten bucks? We could… trade."

He was understandably confused. He seemed like he might almost be offended, then shrugged and said, "Sure, we can 'trade'," he laughed. He reached into an inner pocket and pulled out two crumpled Lincolns, then held them out towards me.

I swiped them and held them away from him before extending the jacket to him. Once he took it, I nodded and said, "Thank you, sir."

But before I could run off he said, "What's your name?"

I froze. Nothing in me wanted to tell him, but I heard the name "Jude" come out of my mouth.

"Jude?" He laughed quietly once. "What a fine name. My name isn't quite as nice, but it's still good. It's Michael."

I nodded. "Nice to meet you, Michael. Thanks. See you later!" I waved as I turned to run.

"God bless you, Jude! God bless you!"

I reached my friends breathless.

"You ripped him off, and yet he still thanks you?" David asked.

"What a weird dude, right?" I replied.

"Yeah yeah, what a crazy guy," Thomas said.

David slapped my back. "You're halfway there now, slacker. I didn't think you'd have it in your to charge a homeless guy for a jacket." He laughed. "Come on! Let's go get some more money."

We finally found another lady like Miss Martin, and I labored for her for over an hour while David and Thomas tried to work their own luck. Unfortunately, she "didn't have any cash on her", which was bull because she got cash for several of her returns. As it turns out, David and Thomas also had no luck to work.

When we met up again, I looked at my phone. "David, I gotta be home in seven minutes. Can you get me there in time?"

"Who do you think I am? Of course I can!"

Thomas said, "But we're still about ten dollars short. Can you borrow some from your parents?"

I turned to him. "What are you, stupid? It's December 26th! They just spent a fortune on my kid brothers, and you think they're gonna lend me ten bucks?"

He shrugged. "I guess we're coming back tomorrow."

I shook my head. "How about this: let's forget this place and see if any of the other shops need help with something."

"Not a bad idea," Thomas replied. Then he snapped his fingers. "Why don't we see if Mr. Jackson needs any work done?"

"Mr. Jackson?!" David said.

"It won't happen," I sighed. "He's too stingy as it is. He'd much rather do something himself than pay anybody else to do it. Why else do you think he's always alone?"

Thomas just frowned.

#

At the other end of town, about fifteen miles north of the mall, there were several large blocks with numerous local mom-and-pop

45

shops. Small, signature, unique stores. Exactly the kind I'd like to have. They stayed in the black solely because this town is nostalgic and traditional, and while they were family-owned-and-operated, they appreciated any help they could get. As such, they were a primary target for people like me, those wanting to make a quick buck with little commitment.

The morning of the 27th, David and Thomas picked me up and dropped me off in that district, then went to get breakfast. They somehow figured they could spare a few bucks.

I ran from store to store, desperate for just one task, with no luck whatsoever. Around the blocks I went, darting to and from the various shops, haggling and begging for a quick ten-dollar job.

No matter how I tried, though, I couldn't get anything. Not one shopkeeper was willing to put me to work for even a paltry wage. After about an hour or two of trying, I sat down on a bench to think my options over.

I called David and gave him my location and told him to come and pick me up.

It was December 27th, and if Mr. Jackson was only going to hold the karts for us until the end of the year, that meant I had scarcely three days to make the money.

My parents weren't going to fork over the dough, the local grannies were being stingy, and the store owners were being penny-pinchers. My only other money-making option was to try other small towns in the area, and that would never work. The closest one was over an hour away, and I wouldn't be able to get out there, find a job, get paid, and get back before Mr. Jackson closed up shop on December 30th, much less do it without my parents' knowledge.

I had only one option left: haggling with Jackson himself. That was something that, according to the local folklore, had never been done. Even veteran insurance peddlers and legendary roadmen couldn't get Jackson to budge on a price or buy something he didn't want. That's why he was called "Stonewall Jackson" by sales reps. Eventually, everyone gave up the idea of selling to Phillip Jackson and he hasn't been bothered by salesmen since.

Needless to say, the odds were against me. But I had no other choice. I steeled myself, gathered my courage, and renewed my resolve. I stood up from the bench, and my confidence exuded from me like an heroic aura.

"Judah? Judah Taylor!"

Those three words shattered my defenses. Rather, it was the voice that spoke my name that did it. I turned towards the sound and saw Michael, the homeless man from the other day, running towards me, wearing the jacket I had sold him.

He stopped when he reached me, breathless. Then he saw the bench and fell upon it.

I stared at him, utterly speechless, while he tried to regain himself. During that time, David and Thomas pulled up. They didn't recognize Michael and David yelled at me to get in the truck, but I couldn't get my feet to move. They were rooted in place, in front of the bench, next to Michael.

He finally looked up at me. "Judah, right?"

Thomas stuck his head out of the car. "Hey, Jude, isn't that the-"

"Yes. Yes it is," I replied slowly.

"We don't have time for this, Jude!" David yelled. "Come on!"

But I didn't hear him. This run-down homeless man had once again captured my attention.

"Jude," Michael said. "You left this in the pocket of the jacket you gave me."

I had no idea what he was talking about. I never wore the jacket, so I definitely never put anything into its solitary pocket. "Surely you're mistaken?" I asked.

He shook his head. "You are Judah Taylor, right?"

I nodded.

"You told me your name was Jude before you left. This envelope was in the pocket." He handed me a plain, white envelope of standard size.

I took the envelope. Sure enough, it had my name on it, and it was written in my father's signature calligraphy. I looked back to Michael.

He panted a bit more and shrugged. "Well, you didn't give me that envelope, you just gave me the jacket. Besides, I assume it's a personal thing, so it's not mine to have."

I realized that he hadn't opened the envelope. "Michael, I <u>sold</u> you that jacket. I didn't give it to you."

He squinted his eyes and tilted his head a bit. He didn't appear to remember or comprehend the way he had been basically cheated just yesterday. Then he nodded and said, "Oh, right. Well, whatever. Either way, this is a nice jacket. I've been looking it over, and it's really unique!"

I grew somewhat bitter, but just nodded. "Right, well, I've gotta--"

He took a closer look at me and said, "Actually, it looks kinda like yours."

I snapped at him. "No it doesn't!" I grabbed a part of my jacket. "Mine's truly unique! I made these modifications myself, not some stupid machine or money-hungry faux-artist! This is my work and my statement!" I spread my arms, showing off my handiwork. "This is my signature!"

Michael walked around me as I said this, examining my handiwork. "Hm. You're right. You're jacket is really cool."

"Don't patronize me!"

He shook his head. "I'm not, not at all. That's about the coolest design I've ever seen. Hammers and lions are a rather odd combination, but they look great." He pointed at the one he was now wearing. "So, what's with this one?"

I could tell that his compliments were sincere, and they placated me. I shrugged. "My parents' sad attempt at making one like mine. I don't know why they took razors to it or bought one with skulls on it. Clearly that's not my style."

He looked at the sleeve. "The skulls look like iron-ons," he said.

I blinked, then dismissed the whole thing. "Whatever. Either way, it isn't my design and it isn't my jacket, so I'm not gonna wear it. That's why I sold it. OK?"

"Your individuality is really important to you, isn't it?"

I took a step back. "What's your point?"

"'Jude' is a pretty Christian name. Are your parents very religious?"

David yelled from his truck. "Crap, Jude! This guy's insane!"

Thomas did, too. "Yeah yeah, nuttier than a fruitcake."

I ignored them. "They're too religious, if you ask me," I said quickly. "But why are you asking me these things?"

His head nodded backwards once, as if he was soaking this all in very deeply. "Ah. So, you don't really like that they make you go to church, and so you skip out a lot. Am I right?"

I took another step back, towards David and Thomas and away from this weird old guy. "Uh, yeah, listen, I'm gonna get going now, so see ya."

He waved me towards him. "Stonewall Jackson's at lunch right now. He said he'd be taking a long one, too, so you've got a minute to talk to an old man."

David revved his truck's engine loudly. "Jude, this dude's messed up! Come on, let's get outta here!"

"Yeah yeah, come on!" Thomas called.

My curiosity won out over my sense of survival. "How did you know I was going there?"

He shrugged. "While I didn't open that envelope, I did read the back." He looked to the sidewalk. "Sorry if that was improper."

I suddenly remembered that I was holding an envelope. I looked back at it and turned it over. My mother had written, "This should convince that rascal 'Stonewall' Jackson to sell you those go-karts! You know what they say, 'money talks'! Love you bunches!"

While I was reading it, Michael said, "And I know about Stonewall because I went there looking for you."

I didn't know which was more shocking: the distance this man walked or his unwillingness to counter-gyp me.

David threw the truck back into gear. "If you ain't leaving, Jude, you're on your own!" With that, he and Thomas was gone, and I was alone with Michael.

I looked back to Michael. "You do know what's in here, don't you?"

He continued to examine his feet. "Probably, yes."

I quickly glanced inside, just to confirm my own suspicions. "There's a hundred dollars in here, and yet you walked over fifteen miles and tracked me down all day to return it to me, after I gypped you for that lousy jacket."

He shrugged again. "I like the jacket," he said.

"Michael, sir." He finally looked at me when I said his name. "Why on Earth would you do that for me?"

He gave an odd half-smile that showed no mirth, but rather great weariness. "Do you want the long answer or the short answer?"

I looked behind me for a moment. "Well, considering my ride just left, the long one's fine." I sat down on the bench beside him. "Tell you what, you give me whichever answer you want. I mean, I can at least have a conversation with you as thanks for... well, being a nice guy."

Michael chuckled at that. "You might regret giving an old man permission to talk all he wants. The short answer is this: My Saviour did more for me than I can fully fathom, so the least I can do is show His love however possible to whomever possible."

I didn't really react to this.

He seemed at a slight loss. Then he said, "Oh, right, 'overly'-religious background. That probably seemed like a cliché answer to you, didn't it?"

I slowly nodded, not wanting to offend him.

"That's why that was the short answer. The short answers are rarely interesting, but that one was true, nonetheless." He took a breath, then went on. "The long answer is more like this: My current mission, my calling, whatever label you want to give it, appears to be to walk where God leads me and aid those whom He gives me. I never know where I'm going, I never know who they are, and I rarely even understand that I'm helping someone until it's all over."

I spoke my mind. "That's odd."

Instead of being offended or put out or anything of the sort, Michael nodded. "I agree. It is very odd. I've never heard of anyone doing something quite like this." He turned from me and looked away, but he wasn't looking at anything visible. "Sure, I've heard of an ascetic wandering around spreading goodwill, but he typically had some sort of plan or direction or target or something. I'm basically running on auto-pilot, only it's more like God-pilot or something. I don't even know when this will end or why this started or what the aim of it all is." He paused.

It was a long pause, and I didn't know what to say. I just waited for him to speak again.

He seemed to remember that I was listening to him, and he looked back at me. "I guess it wasn't that long of an answer, huh?"

A thought came to me. "So, wait, you mean that you're a--"

He rolled his eyes. "Yeah, I'm a born-again, Bible-thumping, go-tell-it-on-the-mountain Christian. Yeah, yeah, label me what you will. All I call myself is someone who preaches Christ crucified."

"You don't know of any other Christians that have done what you're doing?"

"Not really, and definitely not to this extent." He shrugged, then smiled. "It's like this is my signature service or something."

And then it dawned on me. "So, not all Christians are the same?"

He raised an eyebrow. "How much of a religious background have you had? Have you heard of Daniel or Gideon or Paul or Lydia?"

Most of those sounded familiar, and I nodded.

"Peter or Esther or Solomon or Philemon?"

I stuck my hands into my pockets and thought about this for a moment. "They were all pretty different, weren't they?"

Michael just nodded.

"And I guess those differences let them do some pretty cool things."

"Indeed. Paul couldn't have done what Peter did, nor Daniel Gideon."

"Huh. Well, I least I know I don't have to turn into some kinda zombie or something."

"Zombie?" His eye grew wide. "I've never heard that one!"

I laughed, but continued thinking for a bit. Michael respected my silence and said nothing.

Shortly thereafter, David pulled up again. "Can't believe you're still here," he said.

Thomas leaned out the window. "Yeah yeah, we thought you'd be dead."

"Now, that's not a nice thing to imply." I stood up from the bench and stretched. "On the contrary, I've never felt so alive."

"Weirdo," David snorted.

I turned back towards Michael. I took my hand out of my pocket and offered it to him. "Thank you, sir. I had a nice conversation."

He shook my hand and said, "Me, too, Mr. Taylor. I'm glad God brought me here and to you."

"Me, too, brother." We ended the handshake, and I climbed into David's car. "Thanks again, Michael." I looked at David and said, "Let's go."

Michael watched us drive off. Once we had turned the corner, he looked into his right hand and saw two crumpled Lincolns.

#

We assumed Mr. Jackson wouldn't still be out to lunch when we got there, so David parked the truck and jumped out almost before shutting it off. "Come on! Now we've got enough money for the go-karts! What are ya'll waiting for?!"

"Yeah yeah, why wait?" Thomas followed David into the shop.

I was left alone in the truck. I stared at the envelope, once again realizing what I was holding. Five Andrew Jacksons were neatly tucked together inside. "Thanks, guys," I said as I ran to catch up with my friends.

David, Thomas, and Mr. Jackson were all waiting for me, the latter of which didn't appear too happy. I stepped up to the counter and laid the envelope on it, face up, so David and Thomas wouldn't see the sappy message on the back.

Mr. Jackson looked down at the envelope, read the two words gracefully written in blue ink, and smiled. He winked at me and then took the envelope. Still smiling, he held out his hand to David and Thomas, who handed him their cash. Three hundred dollars total. "Good job, lads," he said as he patted my shoulder. Or, rather, as he nearly killed me. "They're all yours." He motioned broadly with his left hand, towards a black tarp that clearly had three go-karts underneath it.

David reached it first and grabbed a corner of the tarp. Thomas and I did the same, then we pulled it off in one smooth, uniform motion. Obviously, the go-karts were there, but that didn't make seeing <u>our</u> go-karts any less wonderful. The three identical go-karts were full of gas, polished, and buffed. They also were re-upholstered in our favorite colors and had personalized keys in the ignitions.

We admired our new purchases for maybe a full minute before we heard a gruff voice behind us. "What're ya doing, lads? Drive 'em on outta here! On the double!"

We jumped into our go-karts and drove out of the shop, waving to Mr. Jackson as we did. We stopped at David's truck where he and Thomas loaded theirs into the truck bed, but I was still in mine, idling.

David said, "Well, come on! Lift her in here!"

"Yeah yeah, we gotta take these for a spin!" Thomas added.

I shook my head. "I've got something else I've gotta do first. I'll catch up with you guys later." I waved to them and floored it. The tires squealed and smoked, and I was off, my hair and jacket waving in the wind.

#

Not only did Mr. Jackson fix-up the outside of the go-karts, he gave them a fantastic tune-up, as well, so it handled great and got me all the way to the mall in good time. It felt odd to park a go-kart at the mall, but I was proud, so I welcomed the odd feeling. I ran in to the mall, bought a single item for about eighty dollars, and drove as fast as my little go-kart could take me to the other side of town.

I drove straight to that bench where I had been not even two hours ago. It was right in front of a diner, so I went inside and asked the first waitress I saw, "Did you see a homeless guy out there earlier today?"

"I did, yeah," she said. "He came in, too. Got some food, said he was going north." She shrugged. "Seemed nice."

"Great, thanks!" I ran out, got back into my go-kart, then sped north out of town.

The roads outside of town are windy, and somewhat treacherous when compared to the ones in town. They're bordered by many trees, most of which are not maintained very well, and some extend over the road rather low.

But that was no problem for an expert driver like me, so I wasn't worried. I wasn't even worried when I turned a sharp corner and saw a large branch at eye level. I wasn't even worried when I swerved and barely missed it.

But I was worried when I heard a loud rip as I passed it.

I stopped and looked at my go-kart. What could have ripped on it? Nothing, obviously, so I checked my face, my hair, my pants… nothing was damaged. What was that sound?

53

I drove back to the branch, mostly just to break it off so that wouldn't happen to anyone else, and saw my answer. I realized then that I should have zipped up my jacket once I got out of town. A good and vital section of it, the lower right-hand part of where the zipper would have been, was hung on the end of the branch.

I took the scrap, broke the branch, and drove on.

#

Michael had made much better time than I thought he would have, but I did eventually catch up to him. He heard the engine and quickly stepped off the road, expecting a full-size car. When he turned and saw me, he almost fell over in surprise.

I stopped the engine, grabbed the bag from the mall, and approached him. "You're a fast walker, Mr. Michael, sir."

He laughed. "Again, why do you call me 'sir'?"

"Would you like to make another trade?"

He looked at me out of one eye, obviously confused. "I'm listening."

"I'll give you all that's in this bag if I can have that jacket back."

"I thought you didn't like this jacket."

I sighed. "I don't, but… I can't just give it away. I'm sorry. I need it back."

He grinned. "You know, they have a term for people like you."

"Desperate?" I suggested.

"Yes, but I was thinking of another," he smiled. "Sure, Jude. Let's 'trade' again. The first one turned out to be such a nice event, so I figure, why not have another?"

I handed him the bag, then he took off the jacket and gave it to me. He shivered as he did so.

"Thank you, sir." I said. "You'll be needing what's in there if you're heading north this time of year. It gets much colder up there."

He looked inside the bag. His eyes grew large, as he looked at me.

I shrugged. "I don't like that it's a name brand coat, but it will keep you warm."

Michael shook his head and tried to return the bag. "No, I can't."

I held up my hands away from it. "Sorry, pal, a deal's a deal."

"Jude, I--"

"It's yours." I extended my hand to him. "Deal"?

He looked at it for a moment, then smiled and shook it heartily. "Deal!" He reached into the bag and threw on the coat. He looked down after putting it on and saw an Alexander Hamilton and a scrap of cloth still in the bag. He reached down and picked them up, paying more attention to the scrap.

It was a perfect specimen of my signature artwork: A scrap of a red jacket with no zipper, a hammer-wielding lion, an outside pocket, and a hand-sewn inside pocket.

I got back in my go-kart. "So long, Michael." I started the engine and drove off.

"But, wait, Judah!" He chuckled. "Didn't even let me thank him."

Athanatos Christian Ministries

is proud to present the 2011

Fyodor Dostoyevsky Award

Third Place

To

David Sable

Boone, NC

(Category: 19 and up)

Bio:

David Sable is the father of two grown sons. He lives with his wife Loretta in Deep Gap, a suburb of Boone, NC.

A Good Day

David Sable

When the sun burst through the bedroom, Margaret Lynn Ewing cursed under her breath as she tugged the sheets over her face. She knew she wasn't supposed to curse and mumbled a "Lord Jesus forgive me," but she hoped that God, wherever he was hiding, understood her disappointment. She had hoped that morning would not arrive and that her restful sleep would not end, but it had in fact arrived in spite of her wishes. She thought of not calling Teresa today or telling her that she had gone to church to serve coffee when she in fact stayed home, but she knew that when she pursued such tactics in the past, she was never able to go through with it. She knew she would end up telling the truth.

She lay thinking, wishing it wasn't Sunday, listening to the clinking ceiling fan, and feeling the cool air. Finally, there came an undeniable point where she could no longer tell herself that she was not awake, and she thrust her shoulders forward against desire. She shuffled into the bathroom, brushed her teeth, splashed her face, and then let her nightgown drop to the floor. She stood under the cool water of the shower, believing for a few moments that it was an endless stream, but eventually that same undeniable feeling emerged and she knew she had to let go of that pleasure. She shut off the water and opened the shower door to a bathroom filled with steam.

She pulled her frumpy brown outfit off of the hook in her closet and put it on with mechanical familiarity. The last thing she did before leaving her room was pause and stare at the switch to the ceiling fan. Finally, she lifted her hand and flipped it off, opening the door to the outside where it felt as if the temperature was already rising.

Lake Street was a straight shot from her apartment to the bus stop, but she took care choosing which side of the street to walk on, weighing which sidewalk felt safer, though there was never a sure way to know. She chose the righthand side for there were more streets to cross and thus fewer houses to pass. She began to walk with her face set forward.

She had not chosen well, for only a few houses down as she passed a brick wall was a man on his knees pulling the weeds from a flower bed by the street. His shirt was off and his back poured sweat from the morning sun. Margaret didn't notice him in time, and now it was too late to cross the street, so she picked up her pace.

"Beautiful day isn't it?" said the man to her, "I hope you're doing well."

"I'm fine, thank you very much," said Margaret stretching out the space between words so that her sentence would drag on until she reached the other end of the man's property, curtailing any possibility of further conversation.

Margaret arrived at the bus stop, and within minutes the number 1010 pulled up. The cool air conditioning of the bus swept over her as she flashed her bus card, which was safety pinned to her brown sweater, and examined the seating arrangement. There was only one man on the righthand side of the bus so she took an empty bench on the lefthand side, halfway between the forward and rear exits. She settled in with relief as the bus pulled away and the letters of Tropics Tanning Salon reflected off the windows.

At the next stop, a four-year-old boy burst on to the bus. He ran down the aisle with exuberance. About his pudgy, round head was tied a paper with glued-on cotton balls, and with the boundless zeal of an innocent creature who could conceive of no opposition, he leaped up on the bench in front of Margaret and triumphantly announced, "Baaaaaaaa!"

Margaret felt a smile appear on her face. "You're a sheep," she said.

"Baaaaaa!" said the little boy.

The mother was just getting on the bus. "Joseph, wait," she said while rummaging through a large disordered bag for her bus pass, knocking out a sippy-cup, some loose crayons, and a towel that was stuffed half way into an unzipped side pocket. The bus driver waved her on and she crammed the items back into the bag as the bus pulled away.

"I'm so sorry," said the mother to Margaret as she reached Joseph out of breath, "Sunday school. You know, the good shepherd story. Joseph is really excited. I mean I'm not doing the Sunday school. Someone else is but I just help out. I think. I'm pretty sure. I lost the schedule but we usually serve on the third week so I think. Yeah, this has to be the week."

Margaret patted Joseph on the arm. "You're a good boy," she said.

The bus picked up speed as the mother rearranged the pockets of the bag, taking creased papers out of one section and jamming them into another section, and Joseph bleated out to passersby, completely oblivious to the fact that he could not be seen or heard through the tinted, soundproof glass.

When the bus reached the stop outside the church, Joseph was down the aisle and on his way.

"Joseph, wait," cried the mother as she pulled the bag together and started after him, having to stop to pick up the towel and stuff it back into the bag. Outside the window, Margaret saw the mother catch up to Joseph and hold his hand, whereupon Joseph took the lead and pulled the mother up towards the church.

Margaret stepped off the bus and saw a row of several steps that led up to the church on the crest. To the right was a marquee announcing the sermon "How to Live the Abundant Life." Next to the marquee was a large, painted thermometer with the red halfway filled in under the caption, "Building Fund Goal: 5 Million –We can do it!" Margaret's knees slightly buckled. She turned around, but the bus had departed.

Margaret took one step at a time until she reached the top of the hill. Before her was the door of the main sanctuary, but she turned to the right to a door marked "Fellowship Hall." The room was empty and cool. At the far wall there was a small kitchenette and a serving bar. Margaret went to the kitchenette and pulled out two

58

large cans of coffee – regular and decaffeinated. She measured the coffee, put the filters into the machine, and carefully poured the water. As she was setting out the creamer and sugar, the sound of high-heels tapped from down the hall.

"Margaret," said Penny as she entered the room, "so good to see you. And you are just in time! The service should be ending in five or ten minutes."

Margaret gave a weak smile and continued measuring out the sugar.

"Got everything OK? Is there anything you need?"

"No,"

"Well, OK," said Penny, "I'll leave you to it then. I do so appreciate you."

Margaret's head lowered and she turned away to check the hot, dripping coffee. She set out the plastic stirrers, the napkins, the artificial sweetener, and the cream, and as the coffee finished, she poured it into a plastic serving carafe to stay hot. She started more coffee dripping in anticipation of the rush and took the cookies out of the package and set them in a circle on a large, silver tray. The room was quiet, cool, and peaceful. Everything was calm and orderly.

As if on cue, the door swung open and an army of parishioners poured into the room. They came into the room in search for coffee and human interaction on the way to somewhere else. A younger couple with no kids heard that the apologetics class was inspiring. Another couple heard that the family class was instructive. Husband and wife directed spurts of short sentences towards each other to quickly communicate who picks up what child from children's church and the infant from the nursery and which child should go off to Sunday school. The line formed along the coffee station as people approached the serving spigot and condiments with fresh indecision. They stirred the sugar and creamer several times, prolonging conversation while those waiting looked at their watches.

"Oh Margaret, so good to see you. I'm always so happy when you serve," said the woman in the flower print dress that matched the dress of the squirming daughter at her feet. Margaret mumbled a thank you while she looked down and then turned to grab a full pot of hot coffee and pour the contents into the carafe. She then prepared a fresh filter and coffee and started another pot.

After the first rush of people, the intensity died down. Most went down the hall chatting about kids and family and jobs and sports, relishing the time before the classes began. A few stayed in the fellowship hall and chatted around the tables. Missionary Bob conducted his discipleship talks with a few college students, his booming voice raised much louder than necessary for the three young men sitting beside him.

"The key, my friends, is total victory over sin," said Missionary Bob, "For if you are not living every day a life of total victory, you are just not doing enough."

Margaret reached to grab the coffee pot. She missed the handle and grabbed the base. The heat radiated from her hand and she pulled back in pain. She went to the sink and held her hand under the cool water. She let it run for several minutes and watched the water stream over her red fingers like a bubbling creek washed over her feet after a long, dusty hike in the middle of nowhere in a life that was now so far away. And this creek was flowing to a waterfall that was plunging into a hidden alcove where she and her friend were flinging off their sweaty clothes and jumping in and splashing, the crystal cold water engulfing them and energizing them. And they were jumping in again and again and turning summersaults and swimming as far as they could to the bottom and plunging back up to the top. Then they were drying off on the rock, feeling the cool mountain breeze and falling asleep under the sky on their sleeping bags, looking at the stars a million miles away, feeling so very much alive.

Margaret shut off the tap and dried her hands. By the carafe was Mrs. Taylor, her grey eyes behind a facial of pasty white makeup. She looked intently at Margaret, forcing a weak smile.

"Have you been to the service?" she asked.

Margaret looked down to her feet. "No," she said.

"Well," said Mrs. Taylor, tilting her head and raising her eyebrow, "you really ought to go, don't you think? It would be a blessing."

Margaret smiled awkwardly and smoothed the sugar, but Mrs. Taylor's kept her intent gaze intact. "You do want a blessing, don't you?" asked Mrs. Taylor.

Margaret felt some weakness in her knees. She reached for the cup of coffee stirrers but misjudged and knocked them to the floor. She got on her knees to pick them up. She wanted to stay on her knees forever, but she didn't want Mrs. Taylor to come behind the counter to talk more about the service and why she should go and about getting a blessing, and she wondered why she didn't just stay in bed with the covers over her head and the cool ceiling fan. When she got up, Mrs. Taylor was gone.

When Sunday school let out, the church came through the fellowship hall to throw away their cups and get a last minute refill before heading home or moving into the second church service.

Many smiled and thanked Margaret and told her that she was such a blessing and that her coffee was excellent and that it was so good to see her because she had such a sweet, giving spirit. Margaret turned away and quietly put each item away and washed the dishes. She turned off the coffee pots, wiped the counter, and rinsed out the carafes. When she was done, the room was empty and cool and orderly again.

Margaret headed towards the exit to the outside. She suddenly remembered Mrs. Taylor's piercing stare, and she stopped short. She paused and waited a long time before she began to walk slowly to the entrance to the church service. When she got to the door, it swung open and an usher with a big smile offered her a bulletin.

"Welcome, sister!" he said.

Margaret felt the rush of the warm air from the sanctuary and saw the people pressed into pews. Her hands trembled, and her feet could not move forward.

"No," she said as she turned around abruptly and took the stairs back down to the bus.

At the bus stop sat the young mother. Joseph's round head lay on her shoulder fast asleep, his body sacked over her lap. On the opposite shoulder was the bag. The sippy-cup was lost. Sticking out of the unzipped pocket was a half-colored pastoral scene of sheep by a pool of water with the caption, "He leads me by still waters."

"The sheep is all tuckered out," said Margaret, smiling at the sleeping child.

"Yes," replied the mother, shifting Joseph's weight to get relief from the pain in her arm. "When the little sheep reaches his limit, the shepherd carries him." The cars zoomed up and down the street, stirring up dust and hot exhaust. The mother looked wistfully into the traffic. "I guess we all have to be carried sometimes," she said with a sigh.

When Margaret walked into her apartment, she switched on the ceiling fan. She took off her sweater and lay down on her unmade bed and listened to the clinking fan blades. She made herself a small lunch and ate slowly. As it got to be near two o'clock, she watched the numbers on the digital clock advance minute by minute until it was exactly two. She paused for a long moment and then slowly dialed.

"Hey girl," said Teresa.

Margaret was silent.

"Hey, girl, you there?"

"Hello."

"So how'd it go today?"

61

"I…" Silence.

"Hey, Margie. I know you're on the line. Talk to me."

"I," started Margaret. "I didn't go to the service."

"OK. So what did you do today?

"I only did the coffee."

"So you served coffee to God's people? Hallelujah! That's just what we talked about."

"Yes."

"So how was it? How do you feel?"

"I didn't go to the service."

"Look, we didn't talk about goin' to no service. We get there when the time comes."

"The lady said I should go and I didn't."

"What lady told you you should go?"

"Some lady at the church."

"Look, child. That lady knows nothing about you. You just do what God has you doin' right now."

"But she said it would be a blessing and that I should go but I couldn't."

Teresa sighed. "Listen to me, child. This morning, you got out of bed and got your eyes off yourself and went down there and served others by serving coffee. That was huge, girl. That was huge. And you should be proud of yourself. You don't need to be beating yourself up no way. You just be proud that you took a big step."

Margaret was silent.

"I'm proud of you, girl. Do you feel good 'bout today?"

"I don't know. Nothing feels good."

"I know, child. You've been through a lot. But it will come. One day it will come."

"When?"

"I don't know, but it will. One day. Look, when my daddy took off and me and God had that falling out, well I dried up for real long time. Did all sorts of things and didn't care for nothin' or no one. Then out of the blue I was cleanin' out my grandma's attic after she died. I found this old hymnbook of hers. I flip through it and one of the songs says, 'the heart of the Eternal is most wonderfully kind.' Just that. And I says, 'well, maybe that's true.' You know, 'just maybe.' It wasn't like I was hopping to church or nothin' but maybe my heart just open a crack that God was like that.

"Over the years, I don't know, maybe five years after that, my mind kept going back and thinkin' on that idea. Until one day I says to myself that there ain't no sense in me putting up a fight no

62

more.   Something in me just say, 'God is not like all those things I be scared of and be mad at.'   And that's when the sun began to come up and it began to be a good day.

"How long for you, child?   I don't know.   But I'm praying it will come soon.   Cause the most surprising thing is that when I finally reached to God, I found that he'd been there all the time carrying me along."

Margaret waited silently.

"Well, you hang in there, girl," said Teresa, "Now, what do you plan to do this afternoon?"

"I don't know."

"We talked about it."

"I'm tired."

"So wha'cha going to do?"

"Maybe lie down."

"And do what?"

"I don't know."

"Wha'cha going to do?"

"Maybe watch TV."

"Now you know what I think about that."

"I'm tired."

"I know you're tired sweetheart.   This is hard work, I know. You did a courageous job this morning.   But it ain't going to do you no good sitting by yourself watching trash.   Just trust me and take one more step today to get out of yourself.   I'm helping you to just take one more step."

Margaret Lynn Ewing took a loaf of white bread down from the cupboard.   She tore the slices into small bite-sized portions and put them into a grocery bag.   She paused at the ceiling fan switch, but then shut it off and went out of her apartment.   She went down Lake Street the opposite way from the bus stop.   The road led to a dirt path that led to a lake.   She stood staring at the body of water from a distance.   Finally, she walked to the edge.   She looked around the perimeter and saw that she was alone.   She squatted down and removed one shoe and sock.   She started to put it back on and then stopped.   She went ahead and took off the other shoe and sock.

She tentatively broke the surface of the water at the lake's edge. It was cool and refreshing.   She put her weight down and felt the mud squish up through her toes.   She put her other foot in and felt the water lap up and back over the top of her feet.

The ducks had spotted her and were now swimming towards her.   They gaggled up the banks and surrounded her as she began to distribute the bread.   The ducks hobbled about in a cacophony of quacks and motion and delight, gobbling up the food. The cool lake swept over her feet, and the soft breeze blew through her hair.

As the sun moved from behind a cloud and caught the lake in a shimmering palette of gold, red and orange, she felt joy in her belly begin to rise up to explode on her face, and her arms began to rise towards the heavens. But then she caught herself and stopped. And she wondered at the fearful voice calling her back to her apartment.

Hieropraxis

is proud to present the 2011

Dante Award

To

Bill Vargo

Ambler, PA

Third place

(Category: 19 and up)

Bio:

William Vargo works in the film industry in Philadelphia, PA. His credits include *Marley and Me, The Last Airbender,* and *Limitless*. He writes in his spare time, but hopes to one day bring his hobby and career together.

His parents gave him a strong Christian foundation and instilled in him a love of reading. He earned a B.A. in TV/Film from de Sales University in 2007. The life of St. Francis de Sales, the patron saint of writers, and the philosophy of the Salesians, inspired him to make religion interesting, accessible, and popular through writing.

Vargo is an avid skier and biker and loves board games. He listens to NPR incessantly and highly recommends WHYY's Fresh Air and WNYC's Radio Lab.

Fan of Disgraced Tennis Star
Rescued By Lobsterman

Bill Vargo

Nuns are basically witches. They wear black, they live in covens, I mean convents, and they spend their time chanting and making children's lives miserable. Then, of course, there are the spells. Don't pretend you don't know what I'm talking about. They plant a little time bomb in your head like, "Judge not lest ye be judged," or, "Don't talk to me that way," and then BAM like a yardstick across your knuckles, their words come back with a vengeance.

I've known about this for years, which is why I've avoided those over-evolved penguins ever since I escaped Our Lady of Perpetual Penitence High School. But like I said, those masters of the dark arts have a way of coming back to haunt you.

So a few months ago, I'm sitting in my office, looking for a trophy wife on E-Harmony. I know what you're thinking, but at that point, it really made the most sense. I had a cushy job, a new condo, a Porsche, timeshare, FiOS... Really, what else could a guy want? I worked for an ad agency then, and business was slow. What did I have to lose?

That's when it happened. Out of the blue, Sister Saint Pain-in-the-Neck showed up unannounced. I don't know what she wanted, something about an orphanage. "Here's the thing," I told her. "We'd love to help, but the economy stinks and we're going through every play in the playbook to keep our clients afloat. We just don't have the resources to spare." That sounded pretty good to me. But the nun persisted like some kind of troll from Grimm's fairy tales.

"You certainly seem to have your hands full here." (No lack of sarcasm when she said it.) "But maybe you could help me with some of your personal free time."

Unbelievable. "Sister, I have your info." I flexed her business card between my thumb and forefinger, tempted to shoot it into the trashcan. "I'll let you know if I can help. Unfortunately, I have a meeting to get to." I've always thought that's a good strategy. Don't say, 'no,' just shove them out the door.

"I understand," she said. "Best of luck with your business. The Good Shepherd always provides for his sheep, even when the sheep themselves aren't sure what they need."

66

I don't know how she did it, but that was the curse. That was the grenade she threw. It took me a while to figure out where all of the shrapnel had embedded itself, but the explosion loomed around the corner.

See, the problem was, we mostly did business for real estate firms. Well, business was slow, obviously. They only kept me on because I spearheaded the campaign to bring STD medication into living room. ("Genorex is what it takes/to save your partner from outbreaks." C'mon, it's catchy, and your kid doesn't know what it means anyway.) Unfortunately, it's very easy to saturate that market.

In January, Murdock and Keylon (makers of Genorex), said they wouldn't be able to renew our contract if sales didn't turn around by February. My boss told me I had until then to drum up some new business or I'd be headed out the door with the contract. Since everyone was advertising in prime time now, we'd lost our advantage. We needed something pretty major to turn the tables in our favor. Not good, especially since I had just purchased a new condo. Oops.

If you haven't connected the dots, yet, the nun showed up on February First. An hour and a half later, I was dragged out of my office kicking and screaming. Stupid nun.

To tell the truth, my first day without a job was pretty awesome. I woke up at 9:30, had two mimosas and watched my fifty-two inch plasma TV wearing only my bathrobe. (I didn't even have to close the front of it.) It was great. And just about the time I couldn't think of anything else to Netflix, this amazing news story broke.

Jimmy Madsen, darling tennis prodigy, had been caught with his pants down, literally. He was in a women's rest room "stringing his racket" with a trainer and someone walked in on them. He still might have gotten away with it, except he invited the other woman to join. So much for that career, not to mention the sponsors. Nobody wants to be associated with *that*.

To be honest, I was disappointed. I mean here was a guy who literally had everything. Cars, houses, cash, women (apparently several of those), I even heard that he owned an island somewhere, and all he had to do was play a freakin' game. I could only ever aspire to such greatness. I would even consider Madsen a sort of role model, but he'd really screwed the pooch on this on. All that sponsorship money gone. Poor guy.

Anyway, I was just watching for the entertainment value, but God strike me dead if Sister Saint Pain-in-the-Neck hadn't gotten her favorite omnipotent being involved in this one. Right about the time I was ready to kill the TV and head out to the bar, Fox News had a late breaking story. One of the women who had slept with Madsen came forward. Madsen had given her herpes. This was fate.

My hero, the fallen angel, was probably holed up in some compound, counting pennies. We were both jobless, but I had the key to our future success. Who would make a better spokesperson for Genorex than the carefree lover boy and record breaking tennis champ Jimmy Madsen? I could hear the voice over now, "We all make mistakes, that doesn't mean we have to live with them."

There was just one problem. He'd been on TV for a few days. Naturally everyone wanted to know where to find him, and he was swamped by news crews, paparazzi, groupies, protesting evangelicals, and so on. I called his lawyer's office and made my pitch. They hung up on me before I even mentioned merchandising. And that's really where you make your money. Obviously I had to work that in sooner.

The lawyer's office was in Baltimore, so I hopped in my Porsche and headed straight for 95 South. As a little aside, I don't know if anyone reading this has ever been on south Broad Street in Philly, but you have the unique distinction of being able to park in the middle of the road. So you really have to watch for someone merging into traffic from the left, especially if you're going fifteen over the speed limit.

I don't entirely remember the accident, except that my head killed and it hurt to breath. But when the dust cleared, who waddled over, but Sister Saint Pain-in-the-Neck herself. I'd just like to say here that while I may have been going a little fast, the accident was probably the nun's fault. I never have met a nun who knew how to drive, but whatever.

"Dearie, don't you look a mess?"

I groaned.

"Not now. You just lie there. How on earth could this have happened?"

Fortunately, she didn't seem to recognize me. Unfortunately, that didn't stop her from torturing me until the ambulance showed up.

"I don't want you to worry about a thing. The sisters are fully insured. God may be watching over us, but we're not dummies. Of course, I don't think it will be an issue. Our van's built like a tank. It might not look that pretty, but it always gets us where we need to go. As I always say, the Good Shepherd provides."

As it turned out, I had a concussion and a cracked rib. The physical damage itself wasn't that bad. The destroyed car, lost license, and missed opportunity were the things that really hurt.

When I had started down Broad Street, it felt like everything was coming together. My mission for Madsen had been divinely ordained. It was practically the quest for the Holy Grail. Now I was sitting in a hospital, watching everything I had ever hoped for slowly slip between my fingers.

My only comfort was that the nursing staff had given me some pretty good drugs. And I was more than happy to up the dose when I started thinking too much. But for the first time in my life, the quick, easy fix just didn't cut it.

*   *   *

I was released from the hospital the next day, but it was a couple of weeks until I felt physically well enough to do anything. By that point, Madsen had basically dropped off the face of the earth. My condo was a sea of beer bottles, take out boxes, and unpaid bills. I'd moved my mattress and a wash basin into my living room so I really only had to get up to go to the bathroom. The day I caught myself peeing into an empty beer bottle, I knew things needed to change. If I was going to live the high life again, I needed a source of income, and I knew just who to call.

"Unemployment services, could you hold please."

Bingo!

A few minutes later the operator came back on the line. "Thank you for holding. May I have your name please?"

"John Sangenitti."

"John?"

"Yes, John."

"Temple class of oh one?"

This wasn't good. "Maybe."

"Oh. My. God. John, it's Amanda Knox, how are you?"

"Uh…good. It's been a while." I racked my brain trying to place the name with a face. It was kind of hard because, if I recalled correctly, she wasn't much to look at. But she had the slightest New England accent, and the girl I was thinking of definitely came from Maine. Every other word out of her mouth was lobstah or blueberry.

"Tell me about it," she said. "When was the last time we spoke? The five year?"

"Yeah," I said, "I don't go to those."

"How have you been? What have you been up to?"

"Well, I'm an ad agent."

"Really? Like with the huge loft overlooking Central Park and the Ferrari?"

"Um…I live in Philly, and it's actually a Porsche." …or was.

"That's still totally awesome. Are you married? I'm sorry, that's personal. But I'm just so excited to hear from you."

I had barely opened my mouth before she continued.

"I was for a few years. Things didn't work out. He didn't want to have kids, and I did, of course. But that's okay. I moved back down here from Kennebunkport last year to kind of clear my head." (Definitely the Mainer.) "We totally need to catch up some time. So what's your social security number?"

That seemed odd, even for her. "I'm sorry?"

"Um, well, I need to verify your soc before we can process your claim."

Oops. You get a bad rep if your classmates know you're filing for unemployment. "Since when do you need a soc for Chinese takeout?"

"What?"

"Isn't this China King?"

"No, this is Unemployment and Compensation, five-three-three-*five*." She laughed. "You'd be surprised at how often that happens."

Really dodged a bullet on that one. "That's funny, well, I guess I'll let you get back to work…"

"So if you were calling China King, you must live like right around the block from me."

"Well, I don't know about that," I forced a laugh. "I travel pretty far for a good egg roll."

"It can't be that far. We totally need to catch up."

"Um…"

"I'm headed up to Maine next week to do some repairs on my parent's cottage, but I'll totally look you up when I get back."

"Awesome."

"I know, right. What's better than a week on the coast of Maine? The only thing is, that stupid tennis player owns an island across the way from their cottage so I guess there's a lot of reporters and stuff camped out."

That little bit of information changed everything. "You mean Jimmy Madsen?"

"Yeah. He's owned the place for years, but now I guess he's hiding there and all kinds of unsavory characters are coming up. It's a shame the way some people just ruin things wherever they go. There's a great beach there. You like the beach don't you? What am I talking about? You probably own a beach somewhere. The only thing is, it has one of the largest tide exchanges in the world, so you only have a beach for like half a day."

There was still hope after all. She went on like that for another twenty minutes. Don't worry. I was able to tune most of it out. Although she did threaten to "catch up" with me several more times. I figured I'd burn that bridge when I got to it. As soon as I got off the phone, I drew up a contract, packed my things, and booked it to the airport.

The flight up required a boarding a series of successively smaller but more expensive planes. And don't forget, I was unemployed (and therefore uninsured) during my little hospital stay. So by the time I reached Maine, my credit card was worth as much as an ice cube in the arctic. I thought I'd get by on that old fashioned New England hospitality. But after weeks of dealing with cadres of drudge reporters, paparazzi, and other West Coast types, the locals had run out of icy stares and started throwing cold shoulders. I was screwed.

I walked to the beach where Amanda's family had their cottage. A couple of shady, white panel vans sat by the edge of the road. Amateur photographers and fortune seekers lurked inside, lenses trained on the island, smudges from yesterday's lobster rolls on their bowling shirts. Nauseating.

Just off shore floated the Madsen compound. Surrounded by pine trees, it wasn't giving any information to the paparazzi. Except for the party yacht docked on the south side and the occasional muffled sounds drifting to shore, you'd think it was uninhabited. That lucky bastard. He really did own an island.

I sighed and looked for a place to sit down. There really wasn't a beach. It was a little odd. The houses were like right there on the water. I mean, you could trip and fall in. Then I remembered what Amanda had said. The tide exchange! The island wasn't that far away. Chop off a few hundred yards at low tide, and I could swim it no problem.

I found a part of the beach that was relatively out of sight and waited for the tides to change. The next day, at low tide, I was easily a hundred fifty yards closer (three hundred if you counted the additional shore on the far side) and I hadn't even touched the water. And...I was off! Then back. Little on the cold side.

But at last, I steeled my nerves and dove in. I'd stripped to my boxers and put my clothes in a plastic bag, figuring they'd stay dry and might even serve as a flotation device. Instead the bag filled with water and made the swim that much harder.

After ten minutes I looked up to check my progress. The shoreline had definitely receded, but I couldn't say the island was any closer. At that point, the cold water still felt refreshing. So I pushed on.

Unfortunately, my cracked rib was causing more pain than I had anticipated. I would have made it otherwise. I'm sure. I can do like four laps in the pool at my gym without a break. (And I mean there and back, not one way.) But with the dead weight of my saturated clothes and the rib, it was hopeless. I was cramping and frozen. Breathing hurt. I looked to the island. There was no way I'd make it. The shore was equally far away. I stopped swimming and did my best to curl into the fetal position while keeping my head above water. Hopefully, at least, they'd find my body. This was it.

Well, apparently it takes slightly longer to freeze to death than I'd thought because I actually floated there for like twenty minutes. Then this chugging sound crept up behind me and two huge hands pulled me out of the water. "I'll be damned if this isn't the ugliest fish I eva' caught." I'd been rescued by a lobsterman, of course.

I sputtered a thank you through my chattering teeth. I was certainly glad to be out of the water, but I didn't know how long it would last. The lobster boat sounded like an old lawn mower and looked like a park bench. That is to say, you could see in between the wood slats. How the boat managed to keep the lobsterman above the water line baffled me as he was more giant than man. No doubt Sasquatch and Long John Silver both had branches on his family tree.

Looks aside, he certainly knew how to treat a castaway. Within a few minutes, he had me in dry clothes eating hot chili out of a thermos. "Listen fishbait," Travis (that was the lobsterman's name) said, "Yoah lucky we've been getting warm watah fuh the last few weeks." (That's right, he freaking called fifty degrees warm!) "I don't know whyyah out heah, but maybe ya could tell me wheah ya'd like fuh me ta drop you off."

(So apparently all you have to do to hitch a boat ride in Maine is dive into the ocean.) "Well, I was actually headed over to that island," I said, pointing.

"Ah, Mistah Madsen's island. I suppose he's not expecting you, owah he'd have offahd you a ride on that yacht of his."

"Truth be told, I've had some trouble getting in contact with him, but we have some very important business to attend to."

"Well, yoah not the only one. Just the only one ta jump inta the ocean fuh it."

At that point, I didn't know Travis long enough to parse out if that was an observation, backhanded compliment, or outright insult. "I think my proposition is particularly unique," I offered by way of explanation.

"Just as long as you don't cause him any trouble. I'd hate to be known fuh brining trouble to one of my neighbahs."

That confused me. Amanda had been pretty clear that the locals weren't a fan of the guy. Maybe I'd heard him wrong. "You consider Madsen a neighbor?"

"We sha-eh a yahd, so ta speak." He cocked his head towards the water.

I suppose that was true. There are only so many oceans you can drop your boat in. But for some reason the idea didn't sit right with me. Neither of us said anything for a few minutes as the boat continued to chug towards the island. "I really appreciate this, Travis. If there's anything I can do to thank you…" *Like get you a new boat*, I added in my head.

Travis chuckled. "No. I might not own an island, but the sea provides foah ev'rything I need. Just make shoah ya get a ride back with Mistah Madsen. I have another two dozen traps ta check."

I glanced over at the party yacht. "I'm sure I'll figure something out."

Travis dropped me off near Madsen's yacht, letting me keep his clothes, but now I was on my own. I followed a road from the dock to what could most appropriately be called a villa, something you'd be more likely to see in the Mediterranean than off the coast of Maine. I rang the doorbell, but no one answered. The door was unlocked, so I crept in.

You name it, he had it. Marble floors, projection TVs (plural), recess lighting, bay windows, Jacuzzis, pool tables, skeeball, an intercom system, art that no one understands. He had a freakin' elevator. Everything was in pristine condition. Not a speck of dust in the place, freshly laundered sheets, starched shirts in the closets, a well stocked fridge (and full kegerator!), but it was eerily empty. All forty-three rooms (I counted) had something to make your jaw drop and turn you green with envy, but none of them had even a hint as to where I might find Jimmy Madsen.

I took a seat on a luxurious leather couch in the second living room and thought about my next move. Maybe he'd gone out on an errand. Then I heard a muffled explosion somewhere outside. About a minute later, I heard another. I followed the explosions, irregular but continuous to the far side of the island. There, Jimmy Madsen, disgraced tennis star and my personal role model, was launching Molotov cocktails into the air and blowing them up with a twelve gauge, a manly and impressive past time by all accounts. But something was a little off.

The assortment of pizza boxes, Tupperware, and liquor bottles at his feet didn't really say "high class" the same way his villa had.

Frankly, it looked like my condo right before I'd left it. The liquor bottles, in particular, spoke more to self destruction than self satisfaction, and concerned me more than the fifty degree water I had just been pulled from.

Madsen launched another bottle into the air and fired. He missed, fired again. "Damnit," he shouted. On the third shot, he hit it and the bottle burst into flames, tumbling into the sea. He chuckled, tossed the gun aside and took a swig from a nearby bottle.

Now seemed as good a chance as any. "Mr. Madsen?" I asked.

He spun, nearly landing on his butt. "I sought thew guys were only here on Suesdays." He'd clearly been drinking for a while. "What'stoday?"

"Um...I'm not sure what you're talking about," I said, half to myself. "I'm John Sangenitti. And, first off, I'd like to say that I am a big fan of yours, both professionally and personally. I've always aspired to live the life of the great Jimmy Madsen."

Madsen took another swig from the bottle.

Okay, time for the A-Game. "I'm sorry to bring up a sore subject Mr. Madsen, but it has come to the attention of the public at large that many of your sponsors have pulled their endorsements and that you have well...um herpes. But I think I have a solution that will benefit both of us greatly."

He hiccupped. "Did your boat break down?"

I hadn't really thought of it, but I *was* wearing a lobsterman's hand-me-downs. "No, Mr. Madsen, don't let my clothes fool you. One has to jump through a few hoops to make it to this remote, but breathtaking outpost of yours. I'm an ad agent. I work for Mur-Key, makers of Genorex. We'd like you to be our new spokesperson."

Madsen patted his pockets until he found a box of cartridges. Then he picked up the shotgun and started loading it. "That's a wild plan," he said. "You sheet scoot?"
I had no idea what he said, but it seemed like a good idea to agree. "Of course. All the time."

"Well, water you waiting for?" He waved me over.

I made my way over to him, and he threw the shotgun at me. I'd never touched a gun in my life. I held it like I'd seen movie characters do all the time. He placed a bottle in his little catapult, tied a rag around the top, and lit it on fire with a Zippo. "Whenever you're ready," he said.

I picked the gun up and stared down the barrel. "I'm ready," I said.

Madsen pressed a button and the bottle soared into the air, a trail of smoke following close behind. I did my best to aim and pulled the trigger. It felt like I was in the car accident all over again. A force that had to be similar to raging bull hit me in the shoulder and nearly knocked me over, and I swore I'd broken another rib. It took all of my energy to stay on my feet.

"I think you were a little left," Madsen said, somehow oblivious to the pain I was in. "Here." He took the shotgun out of my hand and fired it until the empty chamber clicked. "Whooee. Guess that's the one that got away." He smacked me on the back sending a new, but comparably crippling sensation through my body. "Try again?" He put a couple more rounds into the gun.

I bent over trying to catch my breath.

"Man, you need a drink." He offered me a bottle of Jack Daniels.

I waved it off. "Painkillers," I whispered.

He offered me another, much smaller bottle. This one labeled Percocet.

I blinked back a tear, starting to question the wisdom of coming out here. "You're taking that?"

"Hell's yeah."

"And drinking that?" I pointed to the whiskey.

"Got to swash it down with thomething."

Lifestyles of the rich and famous.

"Hey, you want to stay for dinner?"

"Sure." I figured it was still in my best interest to be amenable, but I ought to steer the conversation back to business. I straightened up and did my best to catch my breath. "Now, I'm proposing a national campaign. I was the man who made Genorex a household word, just FYI." I let that sink in as I stomached another wave of pain. "But you figure it'll be a quarter mil just to sign, plus a fee for each spot and merchandising. And that's really where you'll make your money. T-shirts, branding, tennis camps…who knows, maybe even a talk show."

"Can you cook? My cheft sleft. I've got food out the wazoo. I just don't know what to do with it."

"Did you hear me?"

"Sure. If you get me twins and a prescription for Viagra, anything you want."

"Um…"

"Fine. They don't have to be twins, but they do have to ble blonde."

There I was, at the Madsen compound, watching him stumble (literally and linguistically) all over himself. I could have him sign any kind of contract I wanted. Forget that. All I had to do was get a two minute video and sell it to the schmuck's back on the mainland, and I'd be set for life.

I reached in my pocket and pulled out the contract I'd drawn up a few days ago. It was in a Ziploc, but, of course, water had still seeped in. As I was separating the pages a small, cardboard square fell to my feet. It looked like a business card. I picked it up. Sisters of the Good Shepherd. I'd nearly forgotten about her.

I was so close to getting exactly what I wanted. And there, in front of me, Jimmy Madsen, the man who had everything I wanted, was trying to balance another cocktail on his skeet thrower. He shouldered the shotgun and toed the release lever. The cocktail fell off and rolled near an open gas can. Madsen fired wildly, squinting into the horizon to find the bottle.

Maybe getting exactly what you want isn't all it's cracked up to be.

"You know, Mr. Madsen, I'm glad we had this talk. I've got to get going, but my people will be in touch with your people."

"You're going?" he said, loading the gun again.

"Uh…heh, heh, just to get the stove warmed up."

"Let me come with you. It's kind of sticky, I mean tickly, I mean tricky." He started towards me, cocking the gun.

"You know, I used to have a stove just like that. I think I'll be okay."

"But food is all about companionship, man. You know that."

I picked up my pace to give myself a little distance.

"Yogi Berra said that. Maybe it was Sinatra." He stumbled. That was my chance. I bolted. As I passed the first line of trees, I heard him say, "You should know, you're Ital…Irish, right?"

No time to straighten that one out. I hobbled to the shore. Running was considerably easier than swimming, but each step brought fascinating new pains. My only hope was that he had left the keys in the yacht. Or maybe there was a life boat or something. But as I approached the dock, I heard the Doobie Brothers pumping out of a crappy radio. Someone was definitely down there. I cleared the ridge to see a dilapidated lobster boat bobbing in the surf. It was Travis! He hadn't left after all.

I jumped in and smiled meekly at him. "I thought you said you were leaving," I said.

"Ya called my bluff," he said. He turned the radio down and revved the engine.

"That guy almost killed me. You consider him your neighbor?"

"Of course. But I nevah said he wasn't an asshole."

*   *   *

76

Lucky for me, Amanda showed up the next day to do some repairs on her parent's cottage. We did a bit of catching up, and she was generous enough to give me a ride back to PA. I came clean about my job situation, and she enrolled me in unemployment. Not only that, but she mentioned that the order of nuns at her church was building an orphanage. They couldn't pay me, but if they got creative with their book-keeping, they could take care of my medical bills.

It was hard for me to say no. After all, I had lost my job, health coverage, the condo, the car, the time share, my license, my savings, well, everything. Things hadn't exactly gone as I'd planned, but I still had my head above water, so to speak. (I don't even need to mention that the nun got what she wanted all along.) Now, I know what you're thinking, could a nationally renown ad agent used to rubbing elbows with high society really get fulfillment volunteering at an orphanage in West Philly? Well, let me put it like this, when the National Enquirer leads with the story "Fan of Disgraced Tennis Star Rescued by Lobsterman," it does wonders for your ego.

Athanatos Christian Ministries

is proud to present the 2011

J.R.R Tolkein Award

to

Elizabeth Russel

SanAntonio, TX

First Place

(Category: High School)

Bio:

Elizabeth Russell lives in Texas with her parents and two younger brothers. She is entering her senior year of high school. She has loved to write for years, and hopes to write more in the future.

The Friend I Didn't Choose

By Elizabeth Russell

The hardships of being Winnie, a seventeen year old social queen

My brother is like algebra and my parent's rules; he just doesn't make any sense. The other day, our parents forced me to invite him to go play mini golf on the island with MY friends, because "Eli really needs to work on a social life" and whatever, and he told me sorry but he couldn't, he had promised to teach our sister Maeve her new piano song. And I said so what, and he said he couldn't disappoint her.

The kid is seven years old, she shouldn't even know what a piano is. But no, Eli needs an accompanist to play all his favorite songs. I guess I'm not good enough to be the pianist anymore.

Anyway, Eli and Maeve spending time together is unhealthy for both of them; he's lost whatever friends he used to have, and she's showing the early signs of Eli-like weirdness. The other day, I told her to please, please, please tell our parents that it was her who left the milk out after breakfast, because I knew she wouldn't get in as much trouble as I would, and she just looked at me and said:

"That would be ill advised, Winnie. You must take responsibility for your own actions."

A regular little *Yoda*. She really is a cute kid. If only I had gotten to her first, she might have turned out all right.

When we were little, I used to play with my brother, but then he got too weird, so I had to move on. I never talk to him at school; half of my friends don't even know we're related. He doesn't even care. He thinks he's so much better than me, always smiling at me in the halls, just to embarrass me. It's okay with me if he wants to be an antisocial outcast; I just want him to leave me alone.

The hardships of being Eli, her outcast of a brother

I know that God has a sense of humor because my sister and I are twins. I seriously doubt that two people more different than me and Winifred ever came into contact with each other. I guess it's not really her fault she's so whiny and mean; she is a girl, after all. But our sister Maeve is only seven, and she's never had a conniption fit in the middle of dinner when our parents told her she couldn't go to her friend's house because she hadn't finished her homework. I guess Winnie is just the irritable type.

Or maybe she's just stark, raving insane, but I don't think so, because every time I pass her in the halls at school, she has at least three hundred people behind her. Maybe they think she's pretty or something. I wouldn't know; she's my sister. She never talks to me at school. I must be an undesirable, because I used to smile every time I passed her in the halls, but she wouldn't even look at me. And at home it really isn't much better. Oh, well, life is hard. At least I can actually name all of my friends: Maeve.

But really, all things considered, I don't mind that Winnie ignores me. It's just one of the hard truths of life. I don't get bored, even though Maeve is my only companion. We live in Port Isabel, Texas, across the bridge from South Padre Island. I can drive down to the beach whenever I want. I like to fish, because I think I want to be a marine biologist. Or a world class rock guitarist. Hey, they aren't mutually exclusive. In fact, I have this great, shamelessly nerdy vision of teaching school children about marine life through song… but I try to keep my dorky dreams to myself. No matter what, I always have Maeve to bring along to the dock or to accompany me on my keyboard. I guess she's kind of my replacement Winnie. Winnie used to want to be my scientific assistant or keyboard accompanist, but not so long ago I noticed that her eyes would glaze over when I read her a National Geographic article or told her the deeper meaning of a song. I figured I shouldn't bore her, so I started teaching Maeve. She's catching on pretty well. So if Winnie would rather pretend I don't exist, she can go right on ahead.

From an oppressed teenage girl

This is the worst day of my life. My parents forced me to skip going to the movies to have "fun" at the beach with Eli and Maeve. So I had to call up my friends and tell them that I had to go to a family event. Real cool. And Steven Jones, this boy who I really, really like is going, so I felt like it was only fitting to mourn for the entire fifteen minutes it took me to get ready.

"Ready, Win?" Eli yelled from downstairs

"NO, ELI!" I screamed, crying my eyes out on my bed. "I'll NEVER be ready!"

"Okay, five more minutes! We'll be in the truck!"

I heard the door slam closed.

"Winifred, they've already been waiting fifteen minutes!" my dad said.

"I DON'T CARE."

"GET OUTSIDE NOW!" Mom barked.

And she marched right up to my room, grabbed my hand, pulled me up, and walked me downstairs and out to the truck.

Maeve was beside Eli in the front. They were both singing along with the radio. I got in beside my sister and slammed the door.

"You had better be nice, Winifred Anne," my mom whispered just before we pulled out of the driveway.

I ignored her and leaned my head against the window. Eli and Maeve kept singing.

"Turn that off, Eli," I said through gritted teeth.

"But this is truly art!" said Maeve.

"Sorry Win, we haven't gotten to Maeve's favorite part yet," said Eli apologetically.

"Yeah, the lotion part."

"No, it's notion, remember?"

"Ocean?"

"Nnnotion."

"Oh, yeah. And that means a feeling, right?"

"Right."

"Is this it?"

"Yes, it's coming after the instrumental part."

"Okay, I'm ready."

"Sing it, Maeve."

"FOR THOSE WHO HAVE A O... LO... NOTION!"

She looked to Eli for approval.

"Yes."

"Have a notion... That it ain't no... um...be glad you're alive! I wanna find one... face that ain't looking through me! I wanna SPIT AT THE BADLANDS!"

"Excellent, Maeve. That's close enough for our purposes."

"Eli, how would someone look through you?"

"It's a metaphor. It means that people don't pay attention to you because for some ridiculous reason they don't like you and don't see that you're actually REALLY AWESOME."

My brother sure is subtle.

From her extremely irritated brother

I admit, I said that last part a little louder than necessary, but Winnie was seriously asking for it. She hates me so much that she cried for fifteen minutes because she had to spend two hours with me?

We got to the beach before Maeve had finished listening to her song a second time. She said she wanted to swim before fishing, so I carried her sandcastle building tools and inner tube while Winnie followed us with her towel.

We set up in our usual spot. Winnie spread out her towel and lay down, to tan of course.

"You ever heard of skin cancer, Win?" I asked.

"I put sunscreen on."

81

"Okay then. Maeve wants to go look for hermit crabs, so we'll be back soon."

"Aw, that's real nice. Wish I could join you."

It took all of my will power to keep from saying something sarcastic. I kicked the sand as I walked out to the water to meet Maeve.

"Carry me!" she said.

I picked her up and balanced her on my side.

"Okay, let's see if I can carry the crabs and you."

"I'll carry the crabs."

"That's what you say every time. Then they come out of their shells."

"And I scream."

"Exactly. Hey, Maeve, you wanna do something fun?"

"Of course."

"I'll leave you here, and I'll swim out a little farther, and you go back and tell Win that I drowned and see if she cares."

"That wouldn't be nice, Eli."

"I know, I know. Never mind."

"It would be a better use of our time to look for wildlife instead."

"Right, Maeve. You're exactly right."

Winnie's take on the situation: Does this mean I don't have to go to school?

I woke up the next day feeling like I'd been run over by a truck. I was so hot, but so cold… the dreaded flu must have caught up with me at last.

"Mom!" I called. I couldn't be expected to help myself in this condition.

I called her two more times, but I didn't really expect her to hear me because her bedroom was all the way downstairs. I forced myself to get up and dragged my poor aching body out of bed and into the hallway. I staggered to the stairs, where Maeve was lying on her face. I screamed and she picked up her head weakly.

"What's wrong?" she asked.

"What happened to you?"

"I don't feel good, so I went to tell Mommy, but I got tired and so I had to stop and rest here."

It was the most pathetic thing I had seen in my entire life. Dad came sprinting up the stairs with a golf club.

"Who's there... What?" Dad stammered, lowering his weapon.

"What happened?" screamed Mom.

Both of my parents looked at the scene. Maeve was still lying in place and I sat down beside her, my energy gone.

"We're sick," said Maeve. "Very, very sick."

Dad put down the golf club and felt our foreheads.

"Yeah, y'all both have a fever," he reported.

"It must be that flu that's going around," sighed Mom. "Let me get you girls some medicine."

"We have influenza?" asked Maeve, her eyes widening.

"I think so, sweetie," said Dad, picking her up.

"Millions worldwide died in the influenza outbreaks of 1918."

"Now how do you know about that?"

Does he really need to ask?

"Eli."

"Don't worry, Maeve. You'll be better in a couple of days."

"I hope so."

"Trust me, you will be."

Dad carried her downstairs and I didn't follow.

"You need to be carried, too, Winnie?" he asked, coming back up.

"Yes."

He laughed.

"I don't think my back could take it."

"Dad, that's a really offensive thing to say to a woman. Didn't your mother teach you anything?"

"Sorry, sorry, I wasn't calling you fat. Fine, I'll try to carry you."

He picked me up and almost tripped on the first step.

"Dad!"

"I've got you, I've got you."

He put me on the couch beside Maeve. She put the remote into my hand.

"You can choose first."

"Thanks, Maevie."

"But if you cared at all, you'd let me watch 'Blues Clues.'"

I sighed and handed her the remote.

"You're giving it back?" she asked, stunned.

"If I had the strength to argue I still wouldn't because I'm going to be sitting here with you all *day*."

"So we should start off on the right foot."

"Yeah, Maeve."

"Okay, then you can choose."

"Maeve, turn the TV on and put it on 'Blues Clues.'"

"You want to watch it?" she asked, with an expression of deep confusion.

"No! I want to start out on the right foot! TURN IT ON!"

"Okay," she said quickly. "I want to start out on the right foot, too."

"I think you should start out on the left foot," said Eli, coming down the stairs. "What're you girls doing?"

"We have influenza, Eli!" cried Maeve, looking to him with terrified eyes. "Do you think we'll make it?"

"Yes, of course, Maeve. Bad bedtime story," he added to me after coughing into his elbow. "I don't feel good either."

"Eli, didn't you hear me screaming?" I asked.

I knew the answer before I asked the question. The kid could sleep through anything. Last year we went to Washington, D.C. on vacation and some fool set off the hotel fire alarm at four in the morning and Eli didn't even wake up. I was sure I had saved his life by screaming his name again and again and shaking him until he finally got up, so I was really kind of disappointed when it turned out that there wasn't a blazing inferno after all.

"Screaming?"

"Never mind."

"I would've helped you if I'd woken up," he said apologetically.

"Never mind. It hurts my throat to talk."

"Okay, sorry."

After everyone left, I spent the longest two hours of my life watching cartoons with my sister. "Blues Clues," "Dora the Explorer," and so much "Spongebob Squarepants"... Then, I heard the front door open.

"WHO'S THERE?" I yelled. It would be so unfair if a robber happened to come on a day that I was even more defenseless than usual.

"Me," said Eli weakly.

He staggered into the room and collapsed between us.

"I think I have it, too."

So this is how it will be. A week of the three of us, sitting on the couch together. This will be a bonding experience.

Eli's take on the situation: But we were just getting to the good stuff in calculus...

"Let's watch 'Star Trek,'" I suggested hopefully, seeing an educational looking cartoon on the TV.

"Okay," said Winnie, strangely eager.

"Okay," said Maeve.

I forced myself to get up.

"Alright, girls, we're going to watch the old movies. Neither of y'all have seen them. Maeve, you really aren't old enough, so close your eyes when I tell you to. And just remember that Spock isn't really dead, so don't cry."

"What?" gasped Maeve.

"You'll see later, okay?"

"Spock is the one with the pointy ears, right?" asked Winnie.

"Yes."

"What happened?"

"You'll see, Win."

It became our project for the week. We made it through the first two, which took us two whole days because one, two, or all of us kept falling asleep in the middle and then we had to rewind so that we would all be at the same part. I think Maeve might have learned a new bad word or two that I forgot was there, but she definitely liked it and I could tell that Winnie was interested even though she didn't say. It was so weird; she was strangely peaceful and so bizarrely amiable. It made being sick tolerable, except when it was time to answer the door for the pizza man. (We had pizza everyday. It's not like you have a lot of options when you feel so bad you can't stand for long enough to make a simple peanut butter sandwich.) We got into a fight about who had to get up and pay every day. I always lost. Winnie kept playing the whole "You're the man, we're just girls," card and the really disgusting part is that Maeve sided with her, but I fell for it every time.

85

Things were going along as well as could be expected. Then, on the third day, Wednesday, we got to number three, the one where they think that Spock dies but in number four you find out that he actually didn't... it's pretty weird, even for someone like me who enjoys "Star Trek" very much. Anyway, I told Maeve over and over that it was coming, but she still cried like a baby, which made her nose run even worse. I *knew* this would happen. When I reached to get her a tissue from the box on the coffee table, I was shocked to see that Winnie was clinging to a pillow, her face smeared with tears. She noticed I was looking and gave me a horrible glare.

"Why did you make us watch this?" she snarled.

"Winnie, it's a movie. Calm down."

"But... Eli..." she stammered between sobs, "the last words... to Captain Kirk! 'I have been... and always shall be... your friend!'"

Maeve started crying even harder.

"My gosh," I groaned. I felt pretty sick that day, so I guess it made me a little less willing to comfort my sisters over the fake death of a fictional character than I usually would have been. "Girls, it's a movie. I think you both need to take a nap."

"Yeah," said Winnie, wiping her eyes. "That sounds good."

What the heck? I was starting to wish that Winnie would get sick a little more often. It made her so... nice.

They were both asleep in a few minutes. I tried to get some English homework done (I always woke up during my numerous naps thinking of how much school I was missing), but I only got through half a page of *The Scarlet Letter* before I fell asleep, too. We missed lunch that day because no one was awake to open the door for the pizza man and the fool just drove off. When we woke up, Maeve was once again reduced to tears by this unfortunate turn. ("Eli, you're supposed to be taking care of us!")

We all felt better the next day, which was a mixed blessing. The good part was that I knew for sure that we would not succumb to the dreaded flu. The bad part was that Winnie was returning to her normal self. So I had to spend to rest of my time as an invalid listening to "This show is boring, let me find one" and "I'm hot" and "I'm cold" and "I'm so sick of pizza, will you pleeeeease make me a sandwich?" (I only capitulated the first time.) I was definitely glad when we were well enough to return to school on Monday.

Winnie: Um, what did you just say to me?

So I finally recovered from the flu, and tomorrow I'm going back to school. But that's not the bad part. Today I was talking to Claire on the phone and just for no reason at all, Mom barges into my room and tells me that I should do something productive, like reading a book.

"But Mom," I said with my hand over the receiver.

"Hang up and ask your brother to drive you to the library right now."

I could see I wasn't getting around this one (Maeve had said too much about our trip to the beach a while back), so I told Claire that I had to go while my mom stood, hands on her hips, with a look of satisfaction.

"Eli!" I yelled, running down the stairs. "I have to go to the library, I need…"

"Okay!"

Eli appeared in the living room, taking his keys out of his pocket. I'd had him at "library."

He was talking about classic literature all the way to the library, but I didn't hear any of it.

"Okay," he said, holding the door open for me. "It would be good to start with Shakespeare. I think you'd like 'Romeo and Juliet' or…"

"Not a chance, let's go to something easier."

He led me to young adult fiction.

"Here," I said, pulling a skinny book from the rack. "This one is fabulous."

"I don't think you want to do that."

"Why?"

"That one definitely has a tragic ending."

"You've read this girly-looking pink book?"

"No, just look at the title."

I did.

"And?"

"The font. Look at that cursive. It's practically a universal truth, Winnie; the fancier the letters, the higher the body count. Here, the unconventional alignment of the letters on this title definitely suggests humor."

He handed it to me, and I swear the thing weighed ten pounds.

"That's way too long!"

I pulled another thin one. He read the summary on the jacket and told me I wasn't old enough. He chose another in the vein of *War and Peace*, and I tried once again to make it clear that it wasn't happening. It went on like this for a while until I told him that I hated reading, I didn't want his help, and he was the biggest nerd in human history. He had a response for this.

"Just because you're too stupid to read without Sparknotes doesn't mean that I'm a nerd because I have a brain! I'm so sorry I said that!"

He looked as surprised as I was; neither of us had called each other stupid since we were about eight. I mean, I've wanted to, but I try to keep a little bit of truth in my insults, and my brother is by no stretch of the imagination stupid. Even though I don't really like him and I know that he's just jealous, I couldn't help but be a little offended.

"You better be sorry!"

I pulled out the book that I had originally chosen, marched to the counter, and checked it out, with Eli shuffling along behind me.

Eli: The sudden downhill spiral

I have just received the single greatest shock of my life. The day started out like any other; so deceptively mundane. I ate my cereal with Maeve, and we sat in the car and waited for Winnie to finish choosing her outfit. She finally came, and sat in the passenger's seat. But something was up. She was mad over the same thing each and every morning; she didn't get to drive. I sided with our parents on that decision; when one of your kids hit two mailboxes in her first week of driving and the other hasn't hit anything at all in a year of driving, the matter of who drives to school is kind of a no brainer. But this morning she didn't say anything about how our parents liked me best and I was a mama's boy and it just wasn't right because she was older (a word of caution: if you ever wind up as the parent of twins and they ask you which one of them was born first, do yourself and everyone around you a favor and say you don't remember because it is just plain annoying to have someone try to lord over you because they have had an entire seven minutes more experience). Anyway, she calmly got into the passenger's seat and I got kind of concerned.

"Good morning, Winnie," said Maeve as I pulled out of the garage.

Instead of the normal "Yeah, whatever," Winnie turned around and smiled at Maeve.

"Good morning, Maeve. Your hair looks pretty."

Maeve's jaw just about hit the floor, and I had to swerve away from the mailbox to avoid ruining my perfect record. Winnie just smiled, pulled her phone out of her purse, and started texting. Glad to have at least one of her morning rituals back in place, I returned my eyes to the road.

"You didn't tell me good morning, Eli," she said.

Is this a dream? I mean, especially after yesterday's library incident. For the first time, I almost felt like I deserved Winnie's normal behavior.

"Uh... Good morning, Winnie."

"Good morning."

She went back to her texting. Who was she texting? Maybe that had something to do with it. I was about to sneak a glance, but didn't want to risk killing her mood.

"So, who're you texting?" I asked, trying to sound casual.

"None of your business," she snapped.

Her phone buzzed, and she looked down at the message and giggled. Oh, no. This could only mean one thing; a boy was on the other end. A boy she didn't want me to know about. I started going through a list of potential suitors in my head, but realized that it could be anyone. I would just have to pay more attention in school.

We got to the elementary school, and I walked Maeve to her classroom.

"Take care of Winnie," she whispered gravely before letting go of my hand.

When I got back to my car, she was still texting and giggling. This was definitely very bad. We didn't talk for the rest of the way to school, and she got out of the car as soon as we arrived. Not another word. Sighing, I shouldered my backpack and followed her into the school.

Winnie: The day I fell in love for real

I couldn't believe that Jake Miller, the super incredible, amazingly cute, ridiculously awesome football player was actually texting me! This is how our conversation went:

"hay winee."

"hi jake!!!!! <3 <3 whats up?! ☺"

"nuthin. ur pritee. cum 2 movees affter skool with mee?"

"YES!!!!"

"ok kool meat u behind skool."

I was so excited I just couldn't help but share my mood with my poor, unfortunate brother and sister. But of course, Eli just had to ask who I was talking to. See, I don't exactly want him to know that I like Jake. Eli is such a goody goody, and I know he would tell our parents. They don't like Jake because a few years ago he got in trouble for driving without a license. But that's in the past, right? Besides, that's not even close to being the worst thing I've heard about at school.

So I went through my whole day happy. I didn't see Jake all day because he's a senior and we don't have any classes together, but I made sure to tell all my friends. I couldn't help but go into a long discussion about it with my best friend Claire because I kind of thought that she liked him, too. What can I say? The same thing had happened to us about a million times, only the other way around.

When the bell rang at the end of the day, I could feel my heart banging so fast I started getting a little worried. Claire and all the other girls followed me out to the back of school to wait.

Eli: The Sacrifice

My last and worst class was PE. The main reason that I hated it was Jacob Miller, that football player who all the girls were obsessed with. I couldn't really see what they found so captivating about him. Simply put, he looked and acted like a blonde gorilla. If that's what it takes to get a girl to like you, I think I'm out of luck. Worse still, he seemed to have singled me out as some kind of a target for his sick games. To summarize, going into the locker room before and after class was like walking into a deathtrap. Really, really hot water in the shower, clothes in the toilet, you know the rest. Today hadn't exactly been a good day for me. First, I tripped on this girl's foot while I was going to calculus. Then, these two girls in of my English class were whispering through my whole, carefully rehearsed presentation. This is exactly what I hate about high school; you can be pouring your heart out and there will still be a couple of fools in the back of the room giggling about their weekend plans. To top it all off, I dropped my soup in the cafeteria, and this fool put someone else's lock on my locker. And we played "flag" football in PE. I don't think everyone understands the whole no contact idea. Needless to say, I wasn't in the mood for Miller to whip me in the back with a towel the second I walked into the locker room.

"That didn't hurt," I said immediately. (It did.)

Did you know that I'm ranked number one in my class? Sometimes my actions betray that. He whipped me again, laughing with his henchmen.

"That doesn't really hurt, Miller," I said. "Physically, it stings a little, but deep down, I wouldn't care if you and your mercenaries got in a line and clubbed me down with your gym bags."

Way to go. Give the pyromaniac some kerosene and matches.

"You know," he said with an evil smile, "that doesn't sound like a bad idea at all. In fact, I think it would be pretty fun."

"Bye then, Miller. Have a nice day and I'll be seeing you."

I turned around and walked out of the gym. I walked a little faster when I realized Miller was following me. Miller? Who's scared of Miller? He could only snap me in half like a toothpick. I threw my backpack down and ran.

The halls were empty, but I could hear him and his buddies behind me. I regretted dropping my backpack; it was my only hope of self defense. Turning down a hall, I remembered the utility closet. With one superhuman rush of speed, I ran to it, threw the door open, and jumped inside, running right into someone else. I would recognize that "Get off of me!" anywhere.

"Winnie, help me!"

"GO AWAY!"

"I can't because Miller, that twisted maniac, is trying to destroy me," I whispered. "Don't attract attention unless you want my blood on your hands."

I noticed for the first time that she had tears on her face, and it dawned on me to ask her why she was hiding in a utility closet.

"What are you doing in here?"

"None of your business. Hiding because Jake dumped me in front of everyone!"

She started crying like crazy.

"SH! Winnie, he's going to find me!"

She tried to control her sobs.

"It was so embarrassing! He said he'd never even liked me!"

I tried to put on a sympathetic tone, even though I wanted to celebrate.

"He dumped you? You were going out with him? With MILLER?"

"Yes! Well, kind of. No, not really. But he's going to ask Claire out now!"

"Claire? But… that doesn't even make sense."

"He said… he said…" she stammered, "he said I've been gaining weight!"

My fear for my own life instantly dissolved. That jerk just called my sister fat. I couldn't just stand by passively.

I threw the door open. Miller and his fan club were walking casually down the hall. So maybe I had imagined being hunted down for destruction. Better safe than sorry, I always say. I saw Winnie watching through the slightly opened door.

"Hey, Miller," I said. "You swine!"

The elite stopped walking, and Miller smirked. It sounded so bad that I kind of wanted to laugh too. He probably didn't even know what "swine" means. I needed to kick it up a notch.

"I heard about what you said to my sister, and you had better apologize to her."

"I had better apologize?" Miller asked over the laughter of the others.

Yeah, he had a point. Like I was going take him in a fight. But I had started up now, and I wasn't finished.

"That is no way to treat a woman! If you have to cut one down so the other will feel better, there's something wrong. Something seriously wrong. With you. You're never getting married if you stay as the same idiotic, immature, insecure, pig headed…"

I had noticed that he was walking towards me the whole time. I really, really wanted to back up, but I stood still. He did have great timing; I had run out of insulting adjectives just as he came close enough to knock my lights out. But really, he could have just given me a good slap instead of a full scale punch to the face.

"Stop it!" Winnie screamed, running out of the closet.

Thanks, sis. Better late than never.

I thought I was probably going to die of a brain hemorrhage later, but I got up off the floor as fast as I could. Which was not very fast. Shoot, two years of braces for nothing. My teeth used to be so straight. So did my nose. Fortunately, Winnie took over from here.

Winnie: The most painful two words in the English language; "I'm sorry"

I strolled up to that dirt bag, swung my purse back, and aimed for his face. Of course, I couldn't reach that high, so it was more like a tap on the shoulder. I had imagined him flying down the hallway and crumpling in a heap, but he just started laughing, along with everyone else. Time to switch to verbal abuse.

"You hit him! Jake Miller, that was uncalled for! You're so awful! I can't believe I ever gave you a second thought! I hope you get put in detention for the rest of your *life*! I'm totally telling!"

"Oh, did y'all here that?" Miller asked his followers. "Winnie's gonna tell her mommy that I hurt her precious brother!"

I had to stop to think of some more insults before I responded to this, more furious than I had been when Maeve used all of my mascara. *All* of it. On one eye, too! That's when I remembered my brother. I guess breaking up is hard to do, but I don't think it's as hard as breaking your face, so I turned my attention to him. He was still standing, but his face was really bloody and he looked like he was about to collapse.

"Can we go home?" he asked weakly.

"Tell your mommy to give him a kiss for me, Winnie!" said Miller as we walked away.

"Shut your mouth, you Neanderthal!" I screamed.

Fortunately, a teacher chose this moment to appear, and after I was sure that Miller would be brought to justice, me and Eli walked out to the car.

We got into our normal seats; him on the driver's side and me on the passenger's. I gave him all fast food napkins that I could find in the glove compartment.

"It's going to be really embarrassing when I go back to school tomorrow," I sighed as he held them to his nose.

"At least you have a nose."

"Don't worry. I'm sure it's still there."

Actually, I wasn't a hundred percent sure. Neither of us said anything for a minute.

"You were right," I said.

"I know."

"Thanks for standing up for me."

"All in a day's work."

"Sorry."

"It's okay."

He leaned out the window to check his nose in the rear view mirror. It still looked pretty bad. He came back in and reapplied the napkins. What could have possibly possessed him to pick a fight with someone who was probably double his weight?

Duty. Brotherly love. Me. *Darn it.* I'd been feeling this emotional apology coming on for a long time. It was going to happen sooner or later... but, as I always say, better later than sooner! I relaxed in my seat, then looked at his nose again. My goodness, that was awful. Okay, here it goes...

"Eli?"

"What?"

"I was looking through you."

He gave me a look like I had completely lost it.

"You know that song Maeve was singing on the way to the beach?"

Now he got it. He just nodded.

"I've been childish and immature," I said. "And a big jerk. And not a good sister. So I'm really, really sorry. And actually, well, I kind of..."

"Keep going."

"You know, I like you. You're my brother... and... you're nice... What I'm trying to say is even if you're right and you never find that pretty, strange, science loving girl and I keep humiliating myself in front of super cute awesome guys, you still won't die alone because I'll be right across the hall from you in the nursing home. Even if Jake comes around someday, I'll always be..."

"Are you *crying*?"

"I'm talking honestly, and it's emotional! If you'll just give me a second..."

I stopped and took a deep breath.

"I'm *saying*, I'll always be your older sister."

He thought about this.

"Older?"

"Seven whole minutes. Okay, I'll always be your twin sister."

He handed me one of the few unbloody napkins, and I tried to wipe the mascara trails from my cheeks.

"I was looking through you, too," he said.

"What?"

"Oh, you know. I just wrote you off as one of those silly, conceited, annoying, self-centered..."

"Okay, okay, I get it."

"And I'm... I'm... sorry too. You know, it never stops being hard to say sorry to your sister. But I really am."

He took the napkins off his face and leaned his head back to try and slow down the blood.

"I think that most people look through the average high school student," he continued. "Actually, the average person. Which is why you need to find someone who looks at you. Just remember, Winnie; to me, you're a door, not a window."

"What?"

"You know, like dad says when we stand in front of the TV? You make a better door than a window? Because you look through a window..."

"You're so weird, Eli."

"You don't have to get me, Win," he said, crumpling the napkins into a bloody ball and placing it at his feet. "It's like Captain Kirk and Spock."

"Yes... you're logical, I'm emotional. But we could be complimentary."

"Exactly. Yet another example of how the world would be a much better place if we just put down our weapons and watched a little 'Star Trek.' Okay, emotional discussion over. We'd better go before Maeve asks if she can call the FBI to report us missing again."

"Oh, I wonder what her teachers think of her."
He sat up straight and put a hand on the steering wheel. I reached for a tissue from the glove box and wiped my nose, then started crying like a baby.

"It's okay,

Winnie. You told me you're sorry and you won't even remember Jake in ten years."

A pause.

"No, you probably will. But it'll be funny then. It'll be a good story."

"Promise me you won't tell anyone."

"I promise."

"Thanks, Eli."

Eli: Happily ever after (I hope and pray)

Then, Winnie had a hundred eighty degree turn around and I was able to fully appreciate her at last. The end.

Well, that's how I thought it would be, but of course, it wasn't. I mean, she apologized. I apologized. She cried. My nose was purple for goodness' sake! But the next day, she was still Winnie and I was still Eli, and I guess I really shouldn't have been surprised when she started texting in the car just like always. Granted, she did respond to my "good morning" a lot better than normal (she answered, and with some interest). I drove on without talking much to Maeve, extremely confused. Did I do something wrong? I tried to be glad that apparently Claire at least hadn't abandoned her, but trust me, it wasn't easy.

After we left Maeve at the elementary school, the car was completely silent. Then, at school, she went to her homeroom and I went to mine. Well, back to the daily grind, I guess. I opened my planner to see what I had for today. Wait, I never use pink sticky notes... Well, I guess God knew what He was doing when He threw the two of us together after all. There it was, stuck on top of my chemistry assignment, covered with purple ink in my sister's handwriting:

"Eli - I have been and always shall be your friend."

Confident Christianity

is proud to present the 2011

Dorothy Sayers Award

to

Brayden Hirsch

Abbotsford, BC. Canada

Second Place

(Category: High School)

Bio:

Brayden Hirsch is a teenage author from Vancouver, British Columbia. Other than working up stories of suspense in well-lit rooms, his passions include spending time with friends and family, being a movie buff, and watching football.

A Train Story

Brayden Hirsch

Watching the kid sit there, with those tiny, pale hands clasped, head bowed and eyes shut tight like some little priest—well, I should've known. God smiles down on his kind.
Guys like me? Not so much.

"And God, bless us and keep us and help the train ride to end fast, so we can see mommy and daddy." He sighed a quick "amen" and dug a spoon into his oatmeal. In a matter of seconds, penitent angel became snorting pig as he devoured his breakfast.

My stomach rumbled, but I didn't hear it over the clatter of the dining car. My gaze soon trailed out the window.

Winter in the Rockies was something I'd never experienced, and so far I wasn't impressed. After all, snow to California was like

97

Elvis to my father and mother—foreign and unwanted. The train wobbled drunkenly onward, through frozen air and gusts of wind so cold that I could see them blowing like billows of smoke.

"More coffee, boy?" came a voice.

Boy? I looked up and bang, my whole world stopped turning, just like that. I found myself staring at the most beautiful girl I'd ever seen—one of the many, many most beautiful girls I'd ever seen, now that I think about it. Definitely the most beautiful waitress I'd ever seen. Blonde hair, pulled back into a ponytail and shimmering in the white light, rolled-up sleeves and a red apron stained with coffee—I would've taken that train to hell and back, if she was on it.

She cleared her throat, and somehow I managed to snap out of my trance.

"Uh, no. I'm not much for coffee, sorry," I said, watching her closely.

Without making eye contact she bent closer, snatched up my mug, and propped it atop her tray, where mountains of crumpled napkins and dirty plates crowded the surface. Her golden ponytail brushed by my face as she whirled around. I sucked in a deep breath, trying to catch the lingering scent of her perfume.

All I smelt was the manure on the old farmer sitting behind me. The dining car buzzed with voices and the clatter of mugs and plates as the passengers ate breakfast. The hundreds of travelers during the war had given this eastbound train to Chicago its popularity, and even pushing ten years after, I couldn't count one empty seat. If I could've, Stubbs and I would never have wound up at the same greasy table as the praying boy and his grandmother.

Speaking of Stubbs.

Sprawled out on his chair, my friend continued to snore in spite of the racket. While most of us greasers actually greased our hair, I'd never seen Stubbs without that black beanie cap, perched on his perfectly round head. I didn't want to. Seemed to me, he was greasy enough, everywhere except for his hair.

I nudged his arm. "Wake up."

He grunted, and his flabby cheeks twisted in a yawn. His breath stunk like curdled milk. "Thanks, Mr. President," he breathed, smiling with his eyes still shut tight. "Glad you liked my hat. God bless Am—"

"Snap out of it," I said, and hit him again.

Stubbs lurched up, looked around, and then sat back. "Still in the mountains," he said. "You know, I don't like snow much."

"Neither do I."

He stretched his arms back, only to hit the farmer behind us in the head, knocking the cigar from his mouth. Stubbs mumbled an apology and his eyes fell onto the boy's red bowl. "Say, Ace. I'm hungry."

"Tell me about it."

"Got any money?"

"Not a dime." The train swung wide around the corner of a mountain so high that clouds devoured its top half, and I leaned forward on my elbows to look Stubbs in the eye. "Kid won't share us a crumb, either."

"You ask him?"

"A while ago, yeah. He ignored me and got on with his praying."

A tired grin played with the corners of Stubbs's dirt-smudged lips. "Well, then, looks like we'll have to ask again." While the frail little grandmother ran a knife through her fried egg and nibbled like a petrified mouse on her dry toast, Stubbs leaned over and gripped the edge of the boy's red bowl. "Hey, kid. You know what happens when you eat too much of this stuff, don't you?"

The boy stopped chewing with his mouth full. "No."

"Well," Stubbs said, winking at me. "A bowl or two a day and your cheeks start puffin' up like you got allergies. Morning after morning, you go through heaps of the stuff, but does it go through you? Naw. You just get fatter and fatter."

His jaw dropped, and while his lips only trembled, his eyes seemed to beg for our mercy.

"Pretty soon you're so fat you can't even walk. No running, no playing. You just sit there at the table, waiting for breakfast. You'll get so fat your parents call the doctor. He shakes his head and puts you on antibiotics. They taste nothin' like oatmeal."

I added, "And to think that it all started with one bowl." In truth, some mornings I'd consume two and a half bowls of oatmeal, and I was skinnier than this little boy. I wasn't about to tell him that, though. Instead I kept my voice as soft and mysterious as I could and said, "So, kid. How many bowls do you eat?"

The rusty spoon clattered to the table. Tears left glistening tracks on his rosy cheeks. He shoved the bowl away, and it skidded to a halt between Ace and me.

We grinned.

As we downed the last couple of bites, my eyes trailed to the old lady at the boy's side. Her wispy gray eyebrows had scrunched into a frown, her little blue hat slanted on her frazzled hair as she gazed from me, to Stubbs and back. But she said nothing.

I shrugged and looked away. Outside, spotless fields of white spread on every side, but I spied a cluster of buildings up ahead. A minute later, we started slowing down.

Finally, we were here. Somewhere.

"Say, Ace," Stubbs said, swallowing the last bite and scratching his head. "What time is it?"

I tugged on the silver chain that dangled from inside my leather jacket, and pulled out my gleaming silver pocket watch. Before I even looked at the time I stroked its smooth, silver edge. The pocket watch was decades old. Once, it had belonged to my grandfather, and before that, his grandfather. Thick layers of rust tainted its silver surface, probably lowering its value by a mile, but it still felt like a fortune to me.

"Almost eight o'clock," I said. "Somehow we're still on time, even in the snow."

Minutes later, the train rolled to a halt beside a wide, ice-plastered platform, where travelers waited like statues of stone, frozen in the snowfall.. Behind the small, wood-walled station towered a few buildings. Smoke unfurled from chimneys across the sea of white roofs. I sighed.

"Well, Stubbs. What do we have, here?"

The farmer behind us turned. "Small town," he rasped. "On the map it's called Macdonald Falls. It doesn't look like much, but there are those who call it home."

"You live here?"

He grunted. "Thank goodness, no. I just ride the train a lot."

Meanwhile passengers were standing, thanking the waitress and grabbing their bags. Eyes still fiery, the old lady across the table slowly unfolded and stood up. Her shriveled little hand reached for her umbrella and the bag at her feet, and with a nod at her grandson she started toward the doors at the end of the car. The boy hurried into his checkered sweater and followed his grandmother away from the table and down the aisle, saying something about finally seeing his parents. Soon most of the passengers had filed out of the dining car, leaving only Stubbs, me, and the farmer behind us.

"Say, Ace," Stubbs said. "We got no more money."

"I know that."

"So, technically speaking, we can't go any further."

"Not without a ticket we can't."

He slumped further into his chair. "Nobody 'round here seems welcome to runaways."

I frowned. "How do you figure? Who knows we're running away?"

"Well, we're alone, we're young, we—"

100

"Nobody knows how old we really are."

"They can tell," Stubbs said. "Besides, that angel who served you coffee has got to be suspicious, us riding a dining car and not ordering anything." A pause. "Why, here she comes."

Sure enough, the angel was shuffling down the aisle, scrubbing at tables and collecting empty plates and mugs as she went. "Last call to get off, boys," she said, ruby lips unsmiling as usual. "Or are you two staying all the way in to Chicago?"

I flashed her a grin. "I'd love to stay on and watch you wait tables all the way to Chicago, honey, but—"

"—you're broke," she finished.

Stubbs moaned. "Is it that obvious?"

"It's obvious that you're a couple of runaways without a penny to your names. Seems to me you're bullies, too. What were you doing, stealing that poor boy's oatmeal from right under his nose? You should be ashamed of yourselves."

"So we're hungry, what's the big deal?"

"Whatever you say," she called over her shoulder as she started away with her tray of dishes. "Just don't come crying to me when they throw you off into the snow 'cause you got no tickets."

I stood up and called after her. "Yeah? What if I have the tickets, right here in my pocket?"

"Not my job to take your tickets," she said. She kept walking, and I slumped back into my seat.

A minute or two passed. New passengers started sauntering into the dining car, chattering amongst themselves. Two old men came in—one had a gray beard with streaks of white and the other a white beard with streaks of gray, and a plump redhead with too much makeup on followed them in. A host of others began to settle into the seats.

"Maybe we'll make it," Ace muttered.

I looked out the window and spotted the little boy and his grandmother, trudging across the white platform as a new gust of wind blasted snowflakes in their faces. Smothered in snow already, the boy raised a hand to his eyes to shield the cloud of white, and his sweater lifted a little.

That was when I spotted it, wedged under his belt.

A chain.

A chain that gleamed silver in the sun.

"Stubbs," I said, jumping to my feet. "You see that? The kid...he's got a watch. It's mine, ain't it?"

His squinty eyes darted to the platform, and he gave a nervous laugh. "I wouldn't bet my life on it, Ace."

"It's mine," I said louder, but no one seemed to notice. "It's mine!"

"Ace, don't you think it could be a different watch?"
His question wasn't halfway finished before I started down the aisle, almost knocking over the unsmiling angel on my way. Steaming coffee splashed from a pot in her hands.

"Hey," she squealed.

For once, I ignored her. When I burst through the door the frozen air hit me harder than I thought—so hard that I could barely breathe, but it didn't matter. Before long I'd jumped onto the platform, and I could feel my shoes sliding on the snow and ice.

"Hey," I yelled, and heard my voice crack. "Hey! You, kid—turn around!"

"Ace, wait up," came a voice from behind me, and I glanced back to see Stubbs, stumbling after me, one hand flapping like the wing of a flightless bird and the other clutching his beanie cap to his head, protecting it from the wind. "Ace, it could've been an accident," he called.

"Accident your hat," I yelled back. I turned back and kept running. "Watch was a gift from my granddaddy, God rest his soul."

"Ace, pipe down!" Stubbs cried.

People were staring, now.

I looked up ahead to see the little boy tugging on his grandmother's sleeve, near the edge of the platform, and they too stopped to see the commotion. I didn't stop until I was at their side. Then I slid to a halt and grabbed the boy by the collar.

The old lady screamed.

"Give it to me," I said.

Tears flooded the boy's eyes, but he remained limp in my grasp.

"Give it to me!"

"What did you take?" the old lady said. It was the first thing I'd ever heard her say.

"He stole my watch." I hoisted the boy off his feet and shook him. "Give it to me! It's under your belt. I know it is. You can't hide it." I dropped him, and he collapsed to his knees.

Rivers of tears flowed down his face. Reluctantly, he retrieved the silver pocket watch. "Here, take it."

Grabbing the chain, I smiled and turned around. What I saw made me cringe. A crowd had gathered on the platform—little old ladies and big, young men with bulging biceps, all of them giving me iron-hard stares. I gulped. "He stole my watch," I said, my voice trembling. "It was a gift from...my granddaddy. He gave it to me when I was little." Before I knew it, I had collapsed beside the boy,

102

and we both sat there and sobbed as frigid winds buffeted our faces.

"He stole my watch," I kept mumbling.

A murmur washed through the crowd, and they started to turn away. I heaved a sigh.

Then, however, the boy piped up. "He stole my porridge!" he declared, and the crowd turned back, even as the train started to inch down the tracks. More murmurs—I saw their lips move, but couldn't hear them over the engine's rumble. "You stole my porridge, and made fun of me," he said.

As the scarlet Santa Fe engine pulled out of the station, leaving two hopeless runaways alone and snowed-in in an unknown town, I swore under my breath. We were stranded here. First it was ten yards away, then twenty, thirty. It picked up speed at fifty. I thought I saw a trail of smoke, spiraling from the windows of the dining car we had only just left, but I blinked and decided it was only my imagination.

"You said I'd get all fat if I ate too much," the boy was saying. "But my granny said that wouldn't happen, 'cause I'm a growing boy."

"So why'd you steal my watch?"

"I didn't steal it. It was on the floor."

Someone in the crowd spoke up. "Just leave the matter be. Take your watch and get out of here, boy."

I was about to argue when I heard Stubbs gasp. I turned, and then it happened, right in front of our eyes.

A screech tore through the air, and a sound like thunder shook the platform. Everyone around me cringed and turned and smelt the smoke on the wind, saw the flames pour from the windows of train cars. In a matter of seconds, half a dozen cars hung off the track, tilted on their sides with smoke billowing everywhere. The Santa Fe engine at the front kept plowing through snow until it was out of sight, dragging the rest of the train away as if nothing had happened.

Everything fell silent.

Then the little boy started crying again.

What happened after that, I still don't know. Time froze, it seemed, and the snowy world around me washed away. Only minutes after the explosion, with tongues of flame still dancing over the tracks, the crimson lights of a fire truck bled onto the snow, and along with a few other young volunteers, Stubbs and I went in to search the wreck for any signs of life. According to the report, published in the local paper that evening, gasoline from the dining car oven had pooled at the back door. When a passenger went outside for a smoke, he dropped his cigar and the explosion began, derailing the last six cars of the train.

One of them, we had ridden.

We emerged with what I remember to be thirteen men and women with sweltering burns. An ambulance carried them to the nearest hospital, but as for the rest? Dead.

Only a half hour of searching passed before they sent Stubbs and I back to the station—apparently dead bodies were too much for teenage boys like us. In reality, I could've been grown-up and old and still would've vomited at the sight of those charred, snow-covered bodies. And vomit I did, off the side of the platform.

I still have no idea how long I sat there in the cold, Stubbs at my side and paramedics crowding all around us, but I remember thinking long and hard about life, about oatmeal, and about the people on that train car.

The waitress, my unsmiling angel. Gone.

The two old men, with gray and white beards. Gone.

The plump redhead with too much makeup. Gone.

Even the fat old farmer behind us never survived. We found his body in the red snow. Gone.

"Why do you suppose we're alive?" Stubbs said, partway through the day when the sun was enormous and white behind the clouds. I didn't answer him, not then—there was nothing to say. I just stared at my feet, my shoes plastered in snow and ice and my legs so cold they were shaking. "I mean, really," Stubbs continued, staring up at the sky. "We should've been on that train, right?"

"We didn't have tickets," I said quietly.

"But we weren't about to get off at this dingy little town."

That was when two brawny men hauled a stretcher by, with another bloody victim sprawled on top. I vomited again. I leaned over the side of the platform until I could vomit no more, and it was only my tears, plunging to the snowy ground below. Then I felt the soft grasp on my shoulder. I turned to see the checkered sweater, wet with snow and tears, of the little boy.

"I…I'm sorry," he said.

Behind him stood his grandmother, hunched and teary, hair speckled with snowflakes, but I saw a smile on her pale lips. Looking at her, then back at him, I forced a weak laugh. "Sorry?" I said. "What for?"

"I stole your watch."

I looked down at the silver chain, like ice in my numb hands. "Aw, kid, you did nothing wrong. We…we're the ones who should be sorry."

"Yeah," Stubbs added, nodding. "I'll buy you some porridge sometime, kid."

He laughed, and I noticed his smile was missing the two front teeth. He ran to his grandmother, leaned up and whispered something in her ear, and returned to Stubbs and I with a question.

"How about we go get something warm to drink?"

Stubbs jumped to his feet. "I thought you'd never ask."

I wiped my tears away and patted the boy on the head. "So long as it's not coffee."

While a chorus of whimpers, moans, and the occasional scream still sounded on the platform, the old lady led us out the crowded doorway of the station, into the main street of Macdonald Falls. Squat wooden shops flanked the road, many of the doorways and windows dark and heaped with snow. On the right, a log-walled hut boasted an elaborate carving of a mug, hanging over one bright, candlelit doorway. Soon I was holding the door open for the three of them, and we sat down with four steaming mugs of hot cocoa. We planned to spend a half hour talking. The boy told us that he and his grandmother had come to Macdonald Falls to see his father, who worked in a nearby mine, and were staying right through Christmas. His mother had passed away from cancer. They listened while we talked of our home in California, and soon our half hour had multiplied.

"Now," the old woman said, after we finally left the coffee shop. She handed me a few tattered bills. "That's for a meal, maybe two. Maybe a night at the local inn."

"Thanks," I said, smiling and shoving the bills into my pocket. "Thanks a lot."

After exchanging hugs with the pair, I looked up. The night sky shone with stars like diamonds, and cold gusts of wind blew silently across the street. I felt my pocket watch, and stared at its ticking hands for one last time. It was getting late. Stubbs waved down a cab for the two of them, and when the old lady climbed inside I gripped the boy by the shoulder.

"Here, kid," I said, slipping the watch into his hands. "I...I don't really use it much, anyway."

Fireworks exploded in his eyes, and a smile blossomed on his face. "Really?"

I grinned. "See you 'round, kid."

All in all, I lost a lot in that trip—I lost my grandfather's precious watch, and more importantly my pride, and when we finally found our way back home all I got were cold glares from my parents and months stuck in my room, grounded—but I gained something precious, too. A memory. Not a day goes by that I don't think of that train. When I go out, I see their faces in the crowds—my unsmiling angel, the little boy, even his grandmother. When someone whistles, I think of that big Santa Fe engine, and when I eat oatmeal, I cringe.

Stubbs flunked high school like everyone knew he would, but I've been to university, now. I'm making money and somehow I've learned to like coffee. I've never stepped on a train, since that day, yet I can't help wonder what my life would be, if not for trains. If not for that little boy. Sometimes I wonder if he still has the watch, if he ever even thinks about me. All I know is that thanks to him and his grandmother, I made it home at last.

We took a bus.

Athanatos Christian Ministries

is proud to present the 2011

John Milton Award

to

Katherine Bland

Girard, KS

Third Place

(Category: High School)

The Last Generation

Katherine Bland

In the corner of a blue room, a tiny baby boy lay quietly in an oak crib. A young blue-eyed, dark haired girl stood over him, smiling sweetly. His coos flowed up to her ears as he stretched his little arms up to her.

"Not now, Carson, I have to go to my first day of kindergarten!" the little girl chirped and turned to skip out of the room. Immediately the baby boy wailed and even as the young girl shut the door and left with her hand clasped in her mother's, she could hear him. The crying would not stop. She couldn't get it out of her head.

Rachel Hart jerked awake in a cold sweat. She had been having the same dream ever since she was five. Lately, it had become more frequent. There was nothing she could think of that would cause this dream. What was that thing behind the wooden bars? It was almost like some mutant miniature version of a human. Nothing she had ever seen looked like that. Any time she broached the subject, her parents offered no explanation. The most they ever insisted was that she must be eating something wrong before bed.

With a groan, Rachel rolled out of bed and stood at the window looking out over 15th Avenue below. It was another miserably foggy, rainy day in Seattle. The scent of freshly baked blueberry muffins wafted into her nostrils from the kitchen, sending her on a mad dash.

"Honey, you look tired." Her mother worried aloud placing the plate of muffins at the center of the table.

Before Rachel could formulate a response, from the head of the table, her father laid down his paper and spoke. "Nightmare again?" Rachel nodded, quickly noting her parents' uneasiness as they exchanged glances.

"Your eighteenth birthday is coming up, honey. Have you decided which organ you want replaced?" Her mother set the napkins at each spot and motioned for Rachel to take a seat.

"I really can't decide." Rachel reached immediately for the muffins and dropped one on her plate. "It's not a matter of not wanting a new organ. I just can't decide what I want. There are so many good options. I can't decide what to replace first!"

"We might be able to offer up a little extra money to get you *two* replacements. Would you like that?" Her father leaned back in his chair looking at her with strong, approving eyes. Rachel nodded in fervent acquiescence, signaling the end of the discussion.

The family enjoyed their conventional chatty breakfast filled with all the gossip her mother could get her hands on and all the legal worries her father was dealing with. After devouring three muffins, more than usual, Rachel retreated to her room. A sudden hush, however, alerted her to the whispers of her parents.

"We can't wait until her eighteenth birthday to have her temporal lobe replaced. It's only a matter of time before she starts remembering and leaves us like Jacob did." Her mother's whisper was strained, and Rachel could tell she was weeping.

Her father cleared his throat. "Liz, this is the only life she's ever known. Jake had the unfortunate circumstance of seeing the horrible way everyone used to live and somehow thought it was better. He wasn't able to make the commitment to this amazing legacy we all have here. Rachel would understand. She would choose this life. We can always have her memories suppressed again."

"We can't keep doing that! She's older now and it doesn't last long enough to be worth it. We will discuss this further." With that, Elizabeth Hart seized her umbrella and stalked out into the hallway to catch the elevator.

Rachel had never heard her parents fight like this. And what in the world were they talking about? She had a strange feeling her dream held more than anyone was letting on.

"And then they were fighting over whether or not to have my frontal lobe replaced or just to suppress my memories, which apparently they've done before! I don't know what's going on." Rachel took a sip of her caramel latte, instantly feeling better, and stared at the two faces of her concerned friends.

"Your mom just sounds stressed. She probably needs a new heart. My mom just had hers replaced, and she's so calm and collected now. It's nice," Scarlet stated trying to reassure Rachel.

"Have you talked to Jake recently?" Shannon inquired. "Maybe he can help you with this a little better than the two of us can."

Rachel sighed. "He never even said bye to me."

That was an atrocious lie. The night he had snuck off into the darkness, Jacob had kissed her forehead and slipped a cryptic note under her mattress that read:

"Truth with me."

He had also managed to get her his new address. He had gone to live among the people the world shunned. They lived in what was left of the trees, among the eastern mountains, in individual houses made of wood or concrete or stone, instead of the steel and glass skyscraper apartment buildings like everyone else. Rachel had never fully understood the reason Jacob had run away. What did he not like? She knew her brother too well to think it was something frivolous, but at the same time, maybe he was just crazy.

"Hey, ladies!" Robbie's voice cut into Rachel's thoughts. The girls quickly moved their chairs together, allowing Robbie, Preston, and Xander to sit down. Rachel could see instantly that Xander was in one of his particularly crabby moods again.

Rachel had known him her whole life. More recently, their lifelong friendship had bloomed into a romantic relationship. They had plans to be married after finishing their coursework. He would go on to work for the transportation department, and Rachel would join her mother as a secretary for her father's law office. Lately, though, Xander had not been quite as excited about their future plans. Rachel knew it had something to do with a 'book', as he called it, his grandfather had shown him. Xander said it belonged to his grandmother who Rachel knew had died foolishly refusing all organ transplants. Her writings, Xander often explained, told of a world where people had wrinkles, got hurt, and died, but were all so happy at the same time. Rachel could not deny how excited he made her with his energy and excitement about living in this world, but she knew better. Where they were now was perfect.

"You okay?" Rachel whispered as the others ranted and raved about the latest news story to pop up on the TV window screen.

"It's my birthday tomorrow," Xander crossed his arms and leaned toward her.

"That's normally something to be happy about."

"No, Rach, it's my *eighteenth* birthday."

"So?"

"I don't want any brand new organs."

"Xander, we've waited for this moment. It's all we live for. How can you not be excited? It's the start of forever!"

His green eyes darkened. "I don't want to live forever."

"Don't you dare start that again! We're supposed to be together. You're not throwing away your life," Rachel ordered as fury boiled within.

"I'm not the one throwing life away," Xander retorted.

"Okay, you two, I don't know what you're fighting about, but chill." Scarlet insisted, her words cutting through the tension.

"It's nothing serious," Rachel smiled and patted Xander on the back as he forced out a smile.

"Head to the usual place?" Robbie inquired, standing up. Everyone nodded in agreement and followed Robbie to the door. As they exited the café, Xander pulled Rachel aside.

"Will you come with me somewhere tonight?" His eyes were pleading; his expression and tone much softer than before.

"I don't know, I can't…"

"I can tell you why you have that nightmare." With those words and his trusting eyes upon her, Rachel was sold.

That night, Rachel packed a bag, told her parents she was staying with Shannon, and snuck off to meet Xander at the park.

"You promise this will explain what my dream is about?" Rachel dropped her bag at Xander's feet as he threw it in the back of his old 2017 Chevy Camaro.

"Yes, absolutely." He opened the passenger door for her, and she stood dumbfounded. "Have you never been in a car before?"

"Well, no. I use the moving sidewalks and the am-track. Cars are so ancient. How is this still running?" Rachel hunkered down awkwardly and plopped into the passenger seat.

Xander took his seat behind the wheel. "They're not that ancient. It's only twenty years old, but it hasn't been driven that much. My grandpa used to drive it before all that stuff was made, and it was his dad's. Obviously they have found better transportation now, but none of them could bear to get rid of it. Since I'm leaving, Granddad told me to take it." Rachel studied Xander's conflicted expression but allowed the silence to envelope them as he started the car and drove them away.

Rachel noted Xander had been driving them toward the eastern mountains for a couple hours now. They were out in the trees where there were roads made of pavement. Xander continued to remain silent allowing Rachel to take in the surroundings of what was once the typical suburbia. To her it looked barbaric. Why did they have lawns and separate houses? Xander kept his eyes on the road, looking for a place to turn around if need be, but Rachel did not object to going further. He took a right onto a heavily wooded driveway and followed the twisting road to a brick two-story house. He stopped the car facing the house as Rachel's face lit up.

"This is my house," she whispered fumbling with the door handle before finally unlatching it. "We all lived here. My whole family." Xander got out and followed slowly behind Rachel as she made her way up to the steps.

"Knock on the door," Xander urged as Rachel felt the smooth wood with the palm of her hand. Before she could ball up her fist the door swung open and her brother greeted her with open arms.

"Jake?" Rachel inquired, unsure who this aged man was.

111

"Yes, Rach, it's me," he replied stepping back so she could get a good look at him.

"But you look so old, older than Mom and Dad," her voice came out in a raspy, unsure whisper.

"Rachel, I'm only twenty-four. Mom and Dad have had so much work done they look twenty years younger than what they are," Jacob replied, watching his sister's expression. "Thanks for finally bringing her with you, Xander."

"No problem. It's almost cutting it close, but she still has a couple weeks," Xander shook Jacob's hand, and Rachel stared at the two wondering how long they had been in contact.

"Both of you come in, there are people I want you to meet." Jacob motioned Rachel inside while Xander lightly pushed her in, following closely.

"Kristen, this is my little sister Rachel. Rachel, this is my beautiful wife Kristen," Jacob announced. Rachel stared in amazement at the woman before her. She didn't seem quite as "old" as her brother, but out here in this world, she was not at all sure about anything. Then Rachel heard the horrid sound, the wailing that she could never escape from when she slept. Jacob recognized the terror in Rachel's face. He had been around when her nightmares had first started. Kristen left the room and stepped back in with a similar version of the tiny mutant Rachel always saw accompanying the bawling in her dream.

Rachel cringed even as the baby stopped crying. "What is that?"

"*She* is your niece, Emma," Jacob replied. Xander stepped forward and cradled the baby girl in his arms. Meanwhile, Rachel stood rooted in place not sure what to think.

Suddenly she found her voice. "So she's human?"

Jacob chuckled, "Yes. Believe it or not, you and I used to look just like her. In fact, this is what you came for, so everyone take a seat and I'll fill Rachel in on what she needs to know." Kristen took Emma back from Xander and led the group into the living room. "Okay, Rachel, are you ready to know the truth?" Jacob asked, settling in the recliner across from her. This time without hesitation Rachel nodded.

Jacob began, "Roughly twelve years ago, scientists made an insane discovery. They found that they could regenerate any and all body parts by using stem cells. Everything was well and good until people realized this meant they could live forever. With roughly five generations left, there was a shortage of food and water. Naturally, the government stepped in and proposed a so-called solution to the problem. Every baby would be killed because they were, and I quote, 'no longer necessary'. That's exactly what happened. With that, there was a huge standoff between those of us who still stood with God and everyone else who wanted to play God. Our generation is the last to ever exist from beginning to end, except here in this place. We chose the normal, not murderous, way of life." Rachel's puzzled expression spoke the words she could not muster.

"Your dream is a memory. A memory of our little brother who was murdered, because our parents wanted to live forever instead. They took Carson on your first day of kindergarten. Then Mom packed up everything we owned, took us to the city to have that part of our memory suppressed, and moved us into the newest apartment buildings. When we came home, we had no recollection of the little boy who had lit up our lives for two years, or the fact that we hadn't always lived in that apartment. I started remembering everything when I was about your age, too. There's only a certain amount of time the memory suppressors work; the older you get, the harder it is to keep them suppressed. I figured out the truth though, Rach. I caught them talking about it, they couldn't lie to cover it up anymore."

"And then you left," Rachel's accusatory voice barely escaped her lips in a whisper.

"Do you understand why?"

"How could you turn your back on Mom and Dad like that?" Rachel was no longer curious; she was enraged.

"They lied! They killed our brother! Their very own son!" Jacob shouted back exasperatedly.

"For good reason, Jake. How else were the rest of us expected to live?" Rachel glanced over at the way Kristen cradled Emma. She seemed to be blocking Emma from Rachel's words.

"We're not meant to live forever. That was never what God intended," Jacob lowered his voice back to a calmer level trying to reach his sister through a different method.

113

Rachel remained silent. She did not know who this God guy was, but he seemed to be the real problem. Anyone who set up her parents in that light was not good. Her parents did not make a mistake. Just because they had not fully explained everything or revealed the complete past did not matter to her. That was their business. They knew what was best. They had the years of experience and all the worldly knowledge.

Xander spoke up softly but firmly, "Do you remember that day at kindergarten? It seems crazy, but I remember it completely. You rushed into the room to announce that your baby brother had said his first word and it was your name. He hadn't been as advanced as normal babies and you were all worried that he wouldn't be able to talk, but he did. Do you realize how great the light shined in your eyes that day? The fact that you were so important to someone so little meant the world to you."

Rachel's mind flashed back to the evening before that first day of kindergarten. She was surprised at how swiftly the memories came streaming back. Carson and Jacob were lying on the floor rolling a ball back and forth. She, of course, was on a rampage trying to decide what to wear to kindergarten on her first day. There was nothing good enough or pink enough and she had stormed through the house crying before flopping down on the couch. Without a sound, Carson had stood up, waddled over to where she lay, and said her name while softly patting her head.

A tear slowly worked its way down Rachel's cheek. She had not cried since that night. There had been nothing to cry over, that she knew about, until now. Her heart began to ache for the sweet little toddler who had brought her that joy and had cared so much. How could her parents have done such a thing? How could the world have turned away from its very essence?

"Rachel?" Jacob whispered trying to bring her back to the present.

"I want to go home." Her words were barely audible. Xander and Jacob exchanged a glance and nodded. They knew this outcome was inevitable. The four remained silent as Xander and Rachel exited the house.

Xander studied Rachel discreetly the whole drive home. She was wrestling with which choice to make, and how her decision would affect everything she knew. They pulled back into Seattle onto 15th Street.

Before Rachel got out of the car, Xander grabbed her arm, "I'm going to live there. I'm leaving later today."

Rachel nodded and with a sly smile whispered, "Okay. Pick me up on your way out. I have to break this to my parents somehow." She slipped out of his car and ran around the corner to her apartment building.

Xander returned roughly seven hours later, his car packed down, but with just enough room for Rachel to bring everything she owned. He entered the apartment building, raced up the seven flights of stairs and knocked on number 719.

"Hello, Xander, how are you?" Mrs. Hart greeted him sweetly, which took him aback.

"I'm here to pick up Rachel," he fidgeted slightly waiting for her to lose her temper.

"She doesn't want to go with you anymore, Xander." Mr. Hart spoke up from behind his wife.

"I'm sorry, Mr. Hart, but we both know that's not true," Xander retorted.

"Rachel, would you like to go with Xander?" Mr. Hart asked smiling wickedly. He pulled the door open wider revealing what was within. With this new perspective, Xander could see Rachel sitting on the couch in the living room, her head bound in a bandage.

"Who's Xander?" Rachel turned toward the door looking bewildered.

"NO!" Xander cried. "How could you do that to her?"

"How could you brainwash her into thinking she wants to grow old and die?" Mrs. Hart's voice was shrill; her eyes ablaze.
Xander shoved his way past Mr. and Mrs. Hart and fell at Rachel's feet. "Rachel, please!"

"Rachel, dear, this is Xander, you've known him your whole life. You just don't remember right now; it's the effects of your surgery. You two will be married soon, though." Mrs. Hart let out a petite nearly maniacal laugh.

Xander picked Rachel up, "No, I'm taking her with me." Rachel struggled but she was too weak to fight off this stranger. As Xander reached the front door, a team of government officials removed Rachel from his arms and grabbed him, pulling him out into the hall.

"Goodbye, son. See you soon." Mr. Hart nodded brusquely shutting the door in Xander's face. He struggled against the men holding him, but they were too many and too strong.

Wisdom's Gate

is proud to present the 2011

William Blake Award

to

Erika Cornelius

Calgary, Alberta, Canada

Third Place

(Category: High School)

Bio:

Erika Cornelius was born in Pretoria, South Africa, where she lived for 11 years before moving across the globe to Canada. It is there that she experienced the reality of loss, and gained through her loss a desire to know the only God who could comfort her and show her purpose. For as long as she can remember, she has been an avid lover of stories, and especially of the way that they can build understanding and offer encouragement to those who need it. She believes that imagination is the road from the head to the heart, the thing that takes what we know and turns it into something we can understand. It is her passion and desire in life to use her storytelling to share the truth about God's love with the world, a concept of which we so often learn, and yet so seldom understand.

She is currently in the midst of finishing her final year of high school, and plans to go on to university in the fall and study inter-cultural ministry, so that she can become a missionary

The Ice Princess

Erika Cornelius

Fire.

Fear.

It was everywhere at once, overwhelming my every sense and thought and emotion. Heat burned intensely, surrounding and engulfing me until I found I could no longer breathe. I could see nothing but the flash of bright orange and red, hear nothing but the sharp crack of collapsing wood. This was a dream that came often to me, one I had grown used to by now. Fire. Too much...fire.

With a quiet gasp, Adelaide blinked open her eyes and tried to breathe, awakened by an unexpected chill to the bone. The world returned to her in a flurry of realizations: there was no fire here in this empty, broken down old shack. A shiver raked down her spine, and she clutched at the thin blanket under which she lay.

Stupid dream, she thought. *It always comes back. Even when it's cold.*

I'd rather be cold.

A creak caught her attention, and she blinked again, turning over in her spot and pushing herself upright. Will stood in the doorway, facing the world outside. He was adorned in gloves and boots and a thin, bedraggled coat that was just the right size for his lanky frame. The wind blew into the shack and ruffled at his short brown hair. Though he continually insisted that he had turned thirteen this past April, Adelaide could not always be certain. Sometimes he looked younger; sometimes he acted older. *But at least he has an age to claim. I don't even know mine. Must be around the same.*

"Will?" She spoke, and he glanced over his shoulder to offer her a smile.

"Well, good mornin' sunshine! Thought ya'd sleep forever, I did."

"Where are you going?" She figured he wasn't just standing out in the cold for the feel of it. His smile brightened.

"Jus' to buy some bread. Don't ya worry, I'll be back soon. Jus' don't come outside--it's awful cold today!" He gave a salute in parting and made to close the door behind him, but she stopped him.

"Wait!" She called, and he paused, brown eyes blinking expectantly. "You're going into town? I'll come with you." He raised an eyebrow and watched her for a moment before shrugging.

"Well, suit yerself, but I'm warnin' ya, it's cold."

"That's okay." She smiled, pulling the blanket up with her. "I'll take this." She twirled in a circle to wrap it around herself, and hurried to flank his side. He watched her with uncertainty, but did not protest.

"Ya know it's a long walk, don'tcha?" He noted as he closed the door behind her. She beamed at him.

"How could I? You never take me with you."

"Didn't think 'bout that one."

Adelaide inhaled the world around her with absolute awe. Just yesterday, everything had been dry and flat as far as the eye could see. Now it was a winter wonderland. She couldn't help but notice the way the snow glittered in the early morning sun, casting off various different colours as it caught and threw the light. It penetrated her tattered boots and chilled her feet, but still it was mesmerizing.

A familiar tune echoed in Adelaide's mind, and as they neared the town, she began to hum it softly. She could not for the life of her recall where she had heard it, but its words lulled her, too distant to remember and too heavy on her heart to ignore. Will plodded ever-so-quietly beside her, his eyes pleasant but clearly focused on some far-off thing. As they reached the outskirts of the town, Adelaide switched from examining her surroundings to examining the people that inhabited them.

The young girl could not say she was at all particularly surprised to see how few of them there were. On a cold day like today, only the homeless and those who could not afford to take a day off work hung around the streets, their watchful and disinterested eyes barely passing over the young pair. They were no more worthy of notice than anyone or anything else in this impoverished district.

As they turned a corner, Adelaide smiled to see two much younger children playing lightheartedly in the snow. They were clearly street orphans, but still too young to know the unpleasantness of their situation. An older boy kept watch over them, his face somber and his eyes suspicious as he watched Will and Adelaide saunter by. Will turned his usual friendly smile on the boy, but received no smile in return. After a while, they neared the heart of the small district, and Will left the girl to amuse herself while he went to buy some bread with the few shillings he had scraped together. He worked for a shopkeeper most weekdays, building and repairing things, as Adelaide understood it. Sometimes he had to work out in the cold, which the girl thought to be fairly atrocious, but he never complained a word about it.

Adelaide shuffled the snow with her feet, clutching the blanket tightly about her shoulders to stave off the cold. Her thoughts drifted as she continued to examine the glint of the white snow in the sunlight, and her imagination conjured up tales of a princess trapped in an evil wizard's ice castle. Halfway through, she changed direction and decided it was better if the princess *lived* in the castle, instead of being imprisoned in it.

Will interrupted her daydreaming.

"Hey, Addie." He began, and she whirled around, startled by his sudden presence. He moved like a ghost sometimes. How long had he been standing there? He was carrying a long paper bag in his hand, which she assumed contained their bread. The boy smiled at her and cocked his head. "What's yer name?"

"Hm?" She blinked at that, confused.

"Yer surname, I mean."

"Oh." Now she understood, though the unexpectedness of the question still confounded her. She paused and glanced away, trying to find the right words to explain her situation. "I... well, I don't know."

"Wha'sat?" There was something in his voice that she could not place, though it remained as friendly as ever. "Whaddya mean ya don't know?"

"Well..." she tightened her grip on the blanket around her. "I don't--I don't remember. Or perhaps I never knew at all. Actually, I don't remember anything from before you found me--except walking far and being hungry. And Adelaide."

"I see." Will replied, turning onto the path that would take them back home with deep thoughtfulness in his eyes. Adelaide bit down on her bottom lip and followed him. After a minute or so of silence, he spoke again. "Ya know, Addie," he said, "I think ya must come from one of those rich places up north."

She blinked at him for a second, her blue eyes filled with confusion.

"*Me*?" She finally responded. "What makes you say that?"

"That right there," Will answered, "Ya talk proper--not like us from the lower districts. Ya must've been taught good." He grinned at her and raised a finger. "'Sides, *Adelaide*'s a real fancy name, not like what we would have down here."

"You can't prove that," she argued, though she refrained from mentioning that 'Adelaide' might very well not even be her real name. It was just the only name that she remembered.

"Maybe, but I'm still pretty sure."

She chewed on her lip and allowed her gaze to drift over the houses that they passed. While she knew that she must have *some* sort of a past, she wasn't too certain she wanted to remember it. The only life she could recall consisted of endless days of wandering, tired and hungry, with nowhere to belong and nowhere to go. Will had found her unconscious near his shack, having fainted from starvation and exhaustion, and taken her in to help her. That had been only a few weeks ago. The two of them lived alone in the shack now, though he had never told her quite why that was. She didn't want to ask what had happened to his family or how he had come to be here.

Will must have seen Adelaide's sudden onslaught of thoughtful displeasure, because he elaborated.

"Ain't that excitin'?" He commented, grinning and nudging her with his elbow. "Maybe ya used ta live in a nice big house with servants and whatnot, and a nice family and all. Who knows, maybe one day ya might find out who ya used ta be and go back to that life. Wouldn't that be nice? Not havin' to hang around this place no more."

"I don't see anything wrong with my current situation," Adelaide commented, and Will raised an eyebrow at her. She looked away. "Besides," she said, fighting to keep her eyes from reflecting too much turmoil. "If my parents could afford to live comfortably, why would they abandon me? Unless they didn't love me. I'd rather be poor than live with rich parents who don't love me."

Will shrugged.

"Don't see how they wouldna loved ya. Maybe they jus' died, or you ran away, or somethin'. Ended up here."

For a second, fire flared in her mind, and she blinked to clear her thoughts of that strange and nostalgic old dream. What did it have to do with anything? No. She preferred not to think too hard on that question. Not just here and now. She shook her head.

"Maybe," she agreed,   and left it at that. Will changed the subject.

"Anyway, you oughta have a surname."

Again with the surname? Honestly... She smirked and raised a hand from under the blanket to brush snow from her blond curls, shivering as the cold air made contact with her bare fingers. She pulled them immediately back into her little burrow of warmth.

As they turned the corner and neared the edge of town, Adelaide caught sight of the children she had seen before. They had switched from their game and were now building something together in the snow. Behind them, the older boy still sat and watched, his eyes deep and unreadable. Adelaide blinked and stopped in her tracks, for the first time considering his appearance and situation. The younger ones wore thick and patched overcoats that were far too long for them, and they had ragged scarves and mittens. Their clothes were old and worn, but would suffice well enough in this weather. The older boy, on the other hand, had none of these things, clearly having passed up on the warmer clothing so that the little ones would not be vulnerable to the chill.

He sat with his skinny arms wrapped around his torso, and his exposed hands, cheeks and ears were red from the sting of ice in the air. His thin shoulders trembled, though by the bitter look in his eyes he seemed oblivious to it.

Adelaide had not realized these things before, and now she found herself astounded that he should sit out here in this weather with such insufficient protection from the intense cold. He would freeze to death! How terrible. Had no one else passed and stopped to consider this?

The boy raised his head and turned his eyes on her, obviously having felt her gaze on him. He scowled.

"You got a problem?" He demanded, and she furrowed her brow. His expression was hostile. "Watcha starin' at?"

She blinked at him and cocked her head.

"Aren't you cold?" She asked, surprised that her voice was still so calm in contrast to how much his unfriendliness had stung her. The boy's scowl deepened.

"What'sit to you?" He snapped. "Leave me alone. No one talked to you." Though, technically, he had.

The little ones had stopped their building to stare at the two.

"Well, now," Will was suddenly beside her, and again she had to restrain from jumping out of her skin. Like a ghost! His voice was friendly, as usual, but it was underlined by a seriousness that hinted he would not stand for trouble from this stranger. "That ain't no way to talk to a lady. She didn't mean no harm."

"What'sa matter with you lot? Pokin' around where it's nobody's business. Git gone."

"Don' mind if we do," Will grinned, reaching out to take hold of her arm. "C'mon, Addie. No use hangin' around this one." He turned to leave, but stopped in confusion when she refused to budge. By the look in her eyes, he saw she hadn't really been paying any attention to his words. After a second's pause, she slipped out of his hold and headed toward the stranger.

Will thought only for a second to protest to her recklessness, but was curious to see what she intended to do. He watched her in interest as she shrugged off her blanket and knelt to drape it over the stranger's shoulders.

"There." She breathed, eyes glowing with satisfaction. "Much better. That thin shirt won't do a thing for you in this weather--you'll catch a cold, or something worse."

The boy, also, was too stunned to respond, and she offered him a reassuring smile before rising to her feet and returning to her place. Will eyed her now with both brows raised, and quietly flanked her side again as they went on their way. For a little while he did not speak, and then, after a few minutes of silence, his expression fell once more into its usual grin.

"Now, ya see?" He said, and she turned to blink at him. His grin widened. "Ain't no one from around here would come up with doin' a thing like that." She was about to protest and point out that he had, after all, saved her when she was starving and fed her and was *still* taking caring of her, but she feared she would not be able to speak without a voice that trembled from the stinging cold. Will was observant, as usual. He saw how she shivered and draped an arm around her shoulders."Just you mind ya don't freeze to death, hm? Ya want my coat?" She shook her head fervently, and he sighed. "Suit yerself...But it's a long walk home, still."

Well, perhaps it was, but she didn't mind so much. She felt better now, knowing that the stranger would not turn to ice by the end of the day, and knowing that she had done the right thing. She glanced at her smiling friend from the corner of her sight and couldn't help but smile a little, too.

Life wasn't so bad, really. Not so bad at all.

Sojourner Leatherwork

is proud to present the 2011

Flannery O'Conner Award

to

David Krall

Scammon, KS

Third Place

(Category: High School)

Bio:

I was born in Wichita, Kansas to loving parents in the year 1994. By the time my family settled in Parsons six years later, a younger sister had appeared and a strong bond with my extended family had developed. Unfortunately, my mother and father divorced several years after the move, but they maintained a cooperative relationship for the sake of their children, whom they had enrolled at St. Patrick's Catholic School. It was at St. Pat's that I discovered my love of writing.

When I graduated eighth grade, I was faced with a dilemma: as St. Patrick's did not offer a high school education, I would be forced to choose a different school in which to enroll as a freshman. I opted for the Christian education provided at St. Mary's Colgan High School in Pittsburg. Last year, I attended Mrs. Dickey's Creative Writing class, an enjoyable experience that has benefited me greatly. As of this summer, I am a Junior at Saint Mary's, and I look forward to another fun, enriching school year this August!

The Game

David Krall

"Jordan! Take cover! Jordan?" In Jordan Ozze's state of heightened sensation, the frantic voice from his headset rang like a siren, jarring him into action. As his legs sprang into motion, he raised his camouflage-sleeved arms to cover his helmeted head. Jordan urged his legs to move faster as a high-pitched whine began to shake his eardrums.

"I read you," Jordan muttered shortly. "You don't hafta tell me twice." Glancing over his shoulder, Jordan could see that he had distanced himself almost fifty meters from his previous position, and he was still sprinting. The whine was growing louder, and a heavy wind shook the trees through which Jordan made his flight. "That thing's gettin' pretty loud. How long've I got 'till impact?"

"I would estimate...um...." The voice paused as Jordan's contact analyzed the situation. "...fifteen seconds," it concluded.

"Dang it! I ain't *that* fast!" Jordan practically spat. "You think ya coulda warned me sooner?" Driven by a greater urgency, Jordan's legs pumped harder, his feet driving again and again into the hard earth. Thud. Thud. Thud.

"You've got twelve seconds," warned the voice in his ear. Jordan shielded his face with his right forearm, just barely deflecting a leafy branch. He stumbled slightly, but continued his hasty progress. *I can't slow down, even for a second,* Jordan reminded himself. The slightest hesitation, he knew, could make the difference between life and death, and Jordan knew better than to take chances in such situations.

"Ten seconds."

"I might make it." Behind him, the sound had grown no louder; in fact, it had faded slightly. "I can barely hear the thing. Now, what about our targ-?"

At that moment, a loud report issued from a clump of greenery to Jordan's left. Jordan swore and darted to his right as a bullet whizzed past his head. There was no longer any need for news of his target; the enemy had spoken for himself.

"I heard that. Are you...?" For a moment, only static filled Jordan's receiver as his partner struggled with his words.

"No, he missed." The static seemed to increase in volume. Jordan took this to be a sigh of relief, and he frowned. "That one might not've hit me, but I'm still in danger," he observed darkly. "How much time's left?"

"O-one second!" Jordan's comrade stammered, horrified. Clearly, he had forgotten about the threat that hung so close overhead.

Jordan cursed again. Now, escape was impossible. The whine of the approaching projectile had grown again and was now a massive screech. The communicator clicked and someone shouted in Jordan's ear, but the scream had grown too loud. Jordan could only stand, helpless, as a boom resounded through the trees and a shockwave began to spread from the source of the blast.

Then, another crack disrupted the already-turbulent air. Jordan felt something cold enter his chest, shattering ribs as it went. The sensation was not painful, but when Jordan examined the wound, he saw that blood had already begun to turn his green combat vest black. "Th-they got me," Jordan coughed, though he doubted that his comrade could hear him over the wail. Then, as the explosion began to turn the forest red around him, Jordan collapsed, blackness swirling around the fire in his vision. *This is it, then,* Jordan thought, *this is the end.* Gradually, the redness vanished, giving way to a cool, dark black.

"Game Over," read the enormous pearly letters that filled Jordan's vision. "Your score: 47, 900. Your rank: 879,278 out of 1,579,289 players. Would you like to-?" A list of options and an advanced menu would have followed, but with a savage roar, Jordan began to struggle, flailing wildly with invisible limbs. "Game Over" became "Ga- -ver" as wires became disconnected and pieces of hardware knocked aside. "G-," the system attempted desperately to spell out, but Jordan's hand had at last found the power switch. A flip of this plastic instrument broke a circuit, banishing the last ghostly "G" into an abysmal night.

Slowly, fleshy blinds rose from Jordan's eyes, bringing a foggy sunrise to his aching brain. A fixture embedded in the ceiling above him cast its rays about the tidy living space, which now began to emerge from a nebulous sea of shapes and colors. A bed occupied the far wall, and a desk guarded a closet door to the left. On the right wall stood an entryway, flanked by a lamp and a towering bookshelf.

"Jordan! Jordan? Are you alright in there?" The man's voice that filtered into the room rang with genuine concern, so Jordan answered with as much strength as he could muster.

"'m okay," he groaned.

"You don't *sound* okay." A head covered in the same greasy, chocolate-colored hair as Jordan's appeared in the open doorway, followed by the shoulders, chest, and legs of Harold Ozze. Mr. Ozze's thick shoulders heaved once, a sigh. "Kid, sometimes I worry about you. I know you get real into your games, but your mom and I are just down the hall. All you have to do is holler and we'll be glad to help you out."

Jordan lifted himself shakily from his seat and, turning, saw firsthand the wisdom in his father's proposal. The space around the low, black chair from which he had just risen lay in chaos. Mere centimeters from Jordan's foot, a network adapter sat like a lean-to on its antenna and one of its edges. At an arm's length away from the seat, a massive, obsidian tower lay toppled, its thick AC adapter barely lodged in its respective cavity. This adapter wove and snaked haphazardly across the otherwise spotless floor, arriving by a circuitous route at an outlet in the opposite wall. The black box sprouted other cords like a dark, rectangular head growing so many multicolored hairs. Most of these, disconnected at one end or the other, spilled over the chair and onto the floor. A few, however, stretched to the edges of Jordan's vision, pulled taut by an unseen force. Feeling the tug of these plastic-coated chains, Jordan raised his hands to his head and removed a domed black helmet.

What a mess! Jordan reflected in disbelief. *I did that?* As he imagined tedious hours spent matching wires and sockets, consulting a manual all the while, a feeling of dread and even remorse began to stir in some corner of his heart. After a moment, however, pride crushed such sentiments beneath its heavy foot and Jordan faced his father with a withering glare.

"I can take care of myself. I'm not five anymore, Dad." Jordan's reply had been harsher than intended, and his father's face took on a disappointed expression.

"I understand, son. You just tell me if you need help... with anything." On shuffling feet, the man departed.

Like that's going to happen, Jordan reflected irritably. *Didn't I just tell you I can take care of myself?* For a moment, he considered repairing the dismantled console, but, again glimpsing the wreckage, thought better of it and threw himself onto the neatly folded sheets that covered his bed. Due to the fatigue created by his in-game experience, sleep was far more achievable than the virtual reassembly of a video game system. Even so, Jordan's fitful tossing did not cease until hours later.

"Hey, Ozze! What'd you do last night, eat a horse?"

"I dunno, but he sure is as big as one!"

"You guys wanna play football?"

"Great idea! Let's bring Jordan; he'll run five yards, then collapse. We won't even hafta tackle him!"

The jokes and laughter followed Jordan through the halls of George W. Bush Middle School. Every student in Jordan's seventh grade class knew that their classmate's weight was a condition contracted by poor lifestyle rather than genetics, and he was teased accordingly. With each verbal blow, Jordan's broad shoulders sank lower and his fists shook more violently. Finally, at the toll of a bell more beautiful than the fifth level theme for "Starship Xeon" (Jordan thought), classroom doors opened and Jordan sought refuge in Mr. Green's World History class. He claimed his customary seat at the back of the room and practically collapsed into it.

"They sure are brutal today." The words came softly, a bit cautiously. Even before he turned to his left, Jordan knew to whom this voice belonged. He had, after all, heard it on many occasions before. This voice had guided him through treacherous African rainforests and around pits of sizzling lava on the planet Darion. Its owner had made even school survivable for Jordan.

"Morning, Ralph," Jordan greeted his friend. Ralph Giovanni smiled and moved his hands to busily straighten the collar of his starched oxford shirt. This was one of his habits, and Jordan disregarded the action.

"Sorry I wasn't more help last night." Ralph's pale face seemed twisted, as though he were in pain. *He must,* Jordan realized, *have worried about that all night! He probably got less sleep than me!*

"Aw, I just died once," Jordan reassured his friend. "You've saved my life hundreds of times."

"Thanks." One of Ralph's hands had ventured upwards and was now moving his large, round glasses up and down the bridge of his small nose. "I'm sorry the other guys are like that," he breathed, suddenly afraid to be overheard. "They make fun of me, too, you know."

"Soon, we'll get back at 'em. I got an idea...," Jordan began, only to be interrupted by Mr. Green's booming voice.

"Ozze! Giovanni! Class has begun!" the teacher bellowed. Snickers erupted from the class as it turned its collective head to witness the source of the commotion.

"I'll tell you about it at lunch," Jordan muttered before hiding his face behind the cover of his textbook.

At a table in the corner of the lunchroom, far from the chattering, shifting quilt of students that covered the less remote benches, Ralph Giovanni awaited his friend's arrival. He was not disappointed. Five minutes after the bell for lunch had rung, an oversized Hawaiian shirt could be seen emerging from the hungry, milling crowd. Ralph's long-time friend puffed into view, his face so red from exertion that his freckles, so obvious when the boy was stationary, were all but invisible.

Without a word, Jordan heaved his legs over the bench and, still panting heavily, dropped his lunch tray onto the table. Ralph remained silent as well. Just as Jordan excused Ralph's nervous habits, Ralph made allowances for his friend's poor physique. After gasping like a fish pulled from its watery home for over a minute, Jordan finally regained his breath and began to speak to Ralph, whose vibrating foot had begun to convey his eagerness.

"Remember how I said I had a plan in History?" Jordan prefaced. Ralph, though he clearly remembered his friend to have used the word "idea," nodded. "When I was runnin' from that missile last night, that guy stopped me by firing over my head. He scared me, but didn't hurt me."

"Uh-huh," Ralph murmured politely, though he failed to appreciate Jordan's logic.

"All we gotta do is show these guys we're dangerous, and they'll leave us alone!" Jordan concluded with a triumphant grin.

"But...how?" By now, Ralph was thoroughly bewildered. This was hardly an idea and even less of a plan.

"What'd they do last night?" Jordan queried impatiently.

"He pulled a gun on you." Ralph's eyes widened as the significance of this fact began to sink in. "You don't mean we're going to...?"

"That's right." Jordan's pride was evident on his face. "If we walk into school tomorrow carrying guns, those thugs'll never bother us again!" This, Jordan stated matter-of-factly, as though it were the fourth law of nature.

"But..." Ralph would have liked to object, to say, "Wouldn't that be dangerous?" or better yet, "I can't take part in something crazy like that." Instead, he concluded with, "Where'll we get them?"

The question brought a frown to Jordan's lips, causing his already-drooping cheeks to sag so that they were in danger of settling onto the colorful, upturned collar of the boy's rumpled shirt. "That's the problem," he replied. "I never go shopping with my dad, so I've got no idea where to buy 'em. I don't think he's got any at home, either."

Ralph breathed a quiet sigh of relief. His father happened to keep a gun safe, but he had no interest in bringing this to his friend's attention. Due to the unavailability of firearms, he had been spared the adventure, glory, and danger of his friend's latest plot, and he was grateful for his narrow escape. The bespectacled youth relaxed and ceased even to finger his collar. Taking advantage of his companion's silence, Ralph attempted to change the subject.

"So, how was-?"

"Oh! I've got it!" Jordan interrupted loudly. Then, at a gesture from Ralph, he lowered his voice. "I've got some old plastic rifles in my closet back home. They don't really shoot, but they look just like the real thing." Ralph tensed again. As Jordan excitedly educated his classmate on the finer points of his plan, Ralph responded with a mechanical "Uh-huh. Uh-huh." Jordan's enthusiasm had carried him far from the reach of discouragement, much as a boat carries its passengers far from the shore. Nothing remained to Jordan but the sea of ideas in which he floated. Ralph, who grew increasingly uncomfortable with each passing minute, knew from experience that any attempt to reach his friend now would be futile.

Fantasies of the next day filled the long, dark subway tunnel through which the steel carriage shot, carrying Jordan home. Thoroughly invigorated, the boy rushed across his apartment's threshold with such haste that his father glanced up from his newspaper and asked, "What's the rush, son?"

Jordan hurriedly fabricated an excuse for his haste. "Ah, just got to the next level on my game and promised I'd meet Ralph online so we could beat it together." The words escaped in one breath, and Jordan feared that his father might grow suspicious.

Despite his son's concerns, the elder Ozze's credulity was absolute. Still, the story failed to fully satisfy the man. "You do that, kid, but I've been thinking. You play those video games so much, I sometimes wonder if you ever come back to the real world."

"Waddaya mean by that?" Jordan's reaction was defensive. Why was his father bothering him with this now?

"There's so much violence in those things, I wonder what you're learning from them."

"But they're virtual reality, and that means it's supposed to be like real life. It can't be worse than stuff I see and hear all the time, can it?" Jordan argued.

"Sometimes I wonder about that but…never mind. You just go and enjoy your game. Sorry I bothered you." His age beginning to show in his slackened face, Harold Ozze retreated behind his newspaper.

Jordan, meanwhile, had already traversed the length of the apartment's only hallway. He flung his bedroom door open and nearly slammed it closed behind him but reconsidered as the door neared its frame. Such a loud noise as the slamming of a door might draw his father's attention, which could in turn impact the success of his plan. Thus, Jordan caught the door's edge deftly with the tips of his beefy fingers and closed it carefully, allowing it to make no noise louder than a soft click.

Now safe from the eyes of his parents, Jordan strode purposefully across the room. His father, he noted, must have fixed his console; it sat in perfect order on the floor to his left. Reaching the far side of the room, Jordan paused to consider the hulking mahogany desk blocking the closet door, then set his jaw grimly and began to push. With effort, he slid his desk about a foot to accommodate for the door's curved path and stopped, sweaty and panting. His bedroom door, it seemed, had stifled the scraping sound that had accompanied the desk's reluctant journey; the radio still blared from the kitchen where his mother prepared the evening meal and his father remained silent and (as far as Jordan could tell) transfixed by his newspaper.

Now, however, the uncertainty that Jordan thought he had outdistanced with his enthusiasm and impulsive reasoning had finally caught up with him. By moving the large, wooden sentry from the spot it had guarded for five years, Jordan had taken his first step into unfamiliar territory. As the boy questioned whether to proceed, his father's words echoed in his mind. "*I wonder what you're learning from those things. I sometimes wonder if you ever return to the real world. You just tell me if you need help...with anything.*"

How hard could it be to open his bedroom door, walk down the hall, and say, "I need your help, Dad," to the man engrossed in the daily news? *Too hard,* Jordan answered himself. *I'm thirteen, old enough to make these decisions for myself. Dad would just make things harder, as usual. And,* he continued, swiftly regaining his old confidence, *this is something* I *have to do. It's the only way I can win respect at school.* Thus encouraging himself, Jordan grasped the doorknob firmly in his hand and turned it but did not open the door. Behind this thin sheet of wood, he knew he would find the two plastic rifles, large black keys to respect and fear. In mere moments, the toy guns would be in his backpack, waiting to strike fear into his classmates' hearts. Jordan pulled on the handle. He could hardly wait.

"I've got 'em," were Jordan's first words to Ralph when he arrived at their designated meeting place (or "rendezvous" as Jordan insisted on calling it). "They're in my backpack." The two boys stood behind a light post about a block from their school. Jordan's grim determination added weight to each word he spoke. Ralph fidgeted.

"You know...." After his first two words, Ralph's volume dwindled. "Do you...do you really think that...this is right?"

"What?!" Jordan practically shouted.

"Never mind." Ralph's pallid complexion had reddened and he immediately regretted having spoken. It was too late, though; the damage had been done. As Ralph's visage acquired a crimson pigment, Jordan's soon shone a royal violet.

"Ralph, we've been bullied since first grade. *First grade*! We oughta be doing way worse to these guys! It's just a little scare: that works in games, so it oughta work in real life. How different are they, anyway?" What Ralph had feared would be a full-scale eruption had been more of an earnest plea, and Ralph took the opportunity to further his point.

"Sometimes I wonder about that." Ralph never realized that he was echoing the words employed by Jordan's father the night before. "And here's another idea: if the world is a game, then who designed the levels? Is there some all-powerful 'Ultimate Programmer' responsible for our world and, if there is, would he like how we're- Hey! Don't laugh at me!" Ralph cried, a bit hurt, for in an action that had banished all tension from the atmosphere, Jordan had begun to chuckle.

"Ha, ha, ha! Whaduz that make you, one of those religious types?" he guffawed. "An 'Ultimate Programmer!' You should listen to yourself." Jordan's laugh had always been contagious, and Ralph soon began to grin sheepishly in spite of himself. This was the same boy Ralph had always known and he had never managed to remain angry with him for long. Jordan radiated an impression that, somehow, the situation would be alright so long as one followed his lead. Ralph believed it.

"Let's not talk about that now." Suddenly, Jordan ceased to laugh, even to smile. "It's like this: when I leave school today, I'm gonna leave with everyone's respect. Now, you can be a part of that, or you can chicken out. What's it gonna be?"

Ralph would have liked nothing more than to ask for more time. A day would have been wonderful, but Ralph would have appreciated even another hour to consider Jordan's question. By this point, though, there was really only one answer, so Ralph met his friend's eyes with difficulty. "Jordan," he began, "I'm your friend. You know I'm with you on this."

"Good. You'll be needing this." Jordan unzipped his backpack and produced a long, black object. Ralph's hand received it and transferred it to his own schoolbag. Then, emerging from their cover behind the light post, the two boys turned and strode towards the school.

"Boys, class has be-." Mr. Green's customary announcement was interrupted by a voice from the back of the room.

"Shut up or I'll shoot ya!" The voice belonged to Jordan Ozze, as did one of the two deadly, black cylinders pointed at his heart. The teacher's speech faltered. The color drained from his face and, in mute submission, he "shut up."

"That's better." Jordan wove among desks and fellow students until he stood behind Mr. Green at the podium. Behind him trailed a pallid boy with white-blonde hair and oversized glasses.

"Who is that?"

"Ralph Giovanni."

"Ralph? How could *he* be doing this?!"

"He seemed like such a nice kid."

The whispers chased each other around the room for ten seconds, at best, but the noise continued long enough to spark Jordan's irritation. "Didn't you all hear me the first time? I've got a gun and I know how to use it. Now *shut up!*" he roared. An uneasy silence blanketed the room. "That's better. Stay in your seats, everyone, and you, sit down," Jordan ordered, indicating his teacher. The older man, his mouth tightly closed, walked to his desk and sat, hands spread innocuously on the dark, hard wood of his workspace. "That's right. This is *my* class now!" At that moment, Jordan realized that he had complete control over the room. He began to laugh, softly at first, then louder and more maniacally until the sound filled the room and reverberated from the walls.

The class observed in stony silence, unimpressed, and Ralph, who stood protectively behind Jordan at the podium, began to feel a bit embarrassed. "Scare them a little" had been Jordan's plan. Much to Ralph's relief, nothing particularly frightening had yet occurred, unless of course someone in the class was phobic of abnormally loud laughter. "Hey, Jordan, can we go back to our seats now?"

Ralph muttered to his laughing friend.

After a moment, Jordan regained control of himself. His reply boomed nearly as loudly as his earlier fit. "Back to our seats? No way! I just got up here! I…." As he spoke, Jordan cast his gaze about the room, watchful for any misconduct. What he saw, instead, was a lone hand raised above a sea of desks and faces. Surprised, he trailed off and sputtered, "Do you have a question?"

"Yes, why…why *are* you doing this?" The girl trembled, staring nervously at the weapon in Jordan's hand. Jordan pointed his rifle at the girl, who emitted a small squeal and ducked her head.

"What's yer name?" Jordan snapped. The girl could no longer meet his eyes. She stared at the classroom's linoleum floor, shaking so violently that the shortest leg of her chair contacted the white surface three times with each word she spoke. Thud. Thud. Thud.

"I-I'm Wilh-helmina J-J-Jones," she barely managed to convey.

Then, Jordan heard a loud, wet gasp.

"Jordan." Ralph spoke firmly. "She's crying. I've known that girl since second grade, and she's terrified of guns. She has been since she was six and her brother's ex-girlfriend brought one to her house. She's never done anything to you. Please, leave her alone."

Jordan scowled and considered it. His goal, after all was to inspire fear. Still, Ralph had a point. Those who really deserved to feel pain were elsewhere in the room. He turned his gun so that its barrel now pointed at a boy in the front row. He was tall, with short, brown hair that (by Jordan's estimate) extended about three centimeters from root to tip. Tough and muscular, the boy twisted uneasily beneath Jordan's gaze. "I'll tell you why I'm doing this." Jordan's voice had grown quite cold and the boy in Jordan's sights shivered slightly from the chill. "It's because people like *you*," he shouted, advancing on the boy, "tortured me every day for six years! But now, it's the other way around. I can make you pay. So tell me," he said to the boy, whose face now shone with sweat, "how would you like…" he paused, "…to *die*?"

No sooner had Jordan spoken this final word, however, than a loud wail split the air. *It's the emergency siren!* Jordan realized to his chagrin. When activated, George W. Bush Middle School's alarm system not only alerted the entire school building to a security concern, but it drew a squad of armed policemen to the scene as quickly as they could be dispatched. *And,* Jordan realized with growing horror, *the police department is right next door!*

"Ralph! What's going on?" Jordan turned back to his friend, only to catch sight of Mr. Green, one of his hands extended beneath the desk's writing surface. *A hidden button,* he realized, *of course!* The teacher's desk must have been equipped with a button for triggering the alarm. *But Ralph was standing next to him the whole time!* "Ralph! Why didn't you stop him?" Jordan cried desperately.

Ralph still stood at the podium, but the barrel of his rifle pointed unthreateningly at the ground. He favored his teacher with a silent nod, then turned to face Jordan. "I'm sorry." Ralph spoke softly, but the quaver in his voice had all but disappeared. "I'm sorry Jordan." Footfalls were echoing in the hall, approaching the room. "But…" The door to the classroom vibrated as the feet approached their destination. "I can't do this." The plastic gun in his hand fell to the floor with a hollow clack.

No sooner had Ralph's rifle fallen to a heavy rest on the classroom floor than the door to the hallway burst open, admitting five black-clad men. Their helmets were dark with visors hiding their eyes. Where Ralph's shirt boasted a breast pocket, the police units' outfits featured "New York City Police Force" in white lettering.

"Nobody move!" The voice from the first of the visitors was oddly distorted, as though he were speaking through a microphone.

"Drop your weapon!"

"Not-a-*chance*!" Jordan bit out through his rage. *That traitor, Ralph! This is* his *fault!* Jordan's thoughts had turned bitter and razor sharp. Now, he had one goal: revenge.

In a swift movement, Jordan's left hand captured the collar of Ralph's white shirt as the fingers of his right wrapped around the trigger of his plastic weapon. The rifle's long barrel was pushed painfully into the smaller boy's rib cage. *Serves him right,* Jordan thought, *I hope it hurts.* "You come after me, and this boy gets it!" he announced aloud.

"Don't worry, officers, it's just a- Oof!" A jab at Ralph's chest with the rifle silenced him, and the voice from the doorway spoke again.

"I said, drop your weapon!"

"Leave now or I'll shoot the boy!"

"I'll give you five seconds to lay it on the-"

"I'm gonna shoot him right now and see how you like it!" Jordan shouted impulsively, but the room drew a collective breath. This, it seemed, was the extent of the police officers' tolerance. The voice from inside the lead officer's helmet ceased to speak, suggesting to Jordan that the officer had indeed been speaking through a microphone. In that moment, each of the five men pulled an identical weapon from a hidden pocket of his uniform. The guns were the size and shape of pistols, but Jordan knew that they were far more impressive than they appeared; he had used them frequently on "PoliceSim: Las Vegas." These were TK-98s, the most powerful handguns carried by United States police forces, and five of them were pointed directly at him. *It's no problem,* he tried to tell his reeling mind. *I've been in this situation hundreds of times before. Thousands!*

But what if- What if I die? The voice that Jordan thought he had silenced the previous evening had returned and with it came fear and doubt. Jordan attempted to push it from his mind.

I've died before! I've been here a hundred times, and it's always been the same. I can take care of myself now!

"Oh yeah?" Jordan shouted, "Well, I'm not scared of you! You just shoot me for all I care!"

"Jordan! No!" Someone was screaming in Jordan's ear, but the alarm blared so loudly that it threatened to drown out the voice. The cry was too late, however, for the police had risen to Jordan's challenge. Though five guns were pointed at him, a single bullet flew from the leader's weapon, spinning as it flew. The report shook Jordan's eardrums, and the shadowy figure's hand flew back nearly a foot in the air. Time seemed to freeze. *If that bullet hits me in the brain, I'm dead. If it hits me in the neck, I'm dead. If it hits me in the heart, I'm dead.* In his mind, Jordan reviewed the list of "kill shots" from the "PoliceSim" game. The outlook was poor and he knew it. *I'll be seeing the "Game Over" screen any second now,* he reflected as he closed his eyes and waited for the bullet he could not avoid to reach his body. *If it hits me in the head.... If it hits me in the throat.... If it hits me in the chest....*

Apparently, "PoliceSim: Las Vegas" was not included in New York City's police training curriculum, for the bullet contacted none of these. Instead, Jordan heard a sickening squelch and a popping sound to his right. *They've got terrible aim.* Jordan grinned slightly. Never did it occur to him that the force that had spared his life had not been poor aim but, instead, mercy.

Then, a sensation that Jordan had never experienced filled his gun hand and quickly spread until it filled his entire body. The feeling was, at first, comparable to the burn he had sustained the previous autumn when he had accidentally placed that same hand onto a heated stovetop. *But this,* he began to realize as the "burning" reached a crescendo, *is way worse.* It was not, after all, akin to touching a hot stove so much as it was similar to dipping his hand into a vat of molten iron. *But...why?* Jordan was shocked. Why had such pain accompanied the blow? He'd been shot hundreds of times in video games. Thousands! Why did the wound hurt now?

Then, Jordan understood. Clearly his father, Ralph, and the nagging voice inside his brain had been right after all. *I'm sorry, Dad, Ralph, Mr. Green,* thought Jordan as tears welled up in his eyes. *I...was wrong.* Then, Jordan was driven to his knees as his body was shaken by another wave of agony.